THE
TEACHER'S
REPORT CARD

THE
TEACHER'S
REPORT CARD
and other inspiring stories

Mary A. Vandermey

mott media
BOX 236, MILFORD, MI. 48042

All Scriptures are from the King James Version of the Bible.

Library of Congress Cataloging in Publication Data

Vandermey, Mary A 1901-
    The teacher's report card, and other inspiring stories.

    1. Christian life—Fiction. I. Title.
BV4515.2.V36   248'.4   77-2790
ISBN 0-915134-42-X

To

The Children

Contents

Spring Inspirations

Final Weeks

Foreword

Our schools are what the teachers make them. To some Americans, an impressive building means a good school. But experience has taught us that schools will never be any better than the teachers in them.

The role of the teacher is of strategic importance, as are many other things. Research tells us that all that is taught stands or falls by the kind of relationship which exists between teachers and pupils. What the teacher is as a person is deeply significant.

Teachers in Christian schools have a dual role to play. They are ministers of the Word and professional persons at the same time. This calls for the very best in them.

Mrs. Vandermey has rendered outstanding service as a teacher in a Lutheran elementary school. Her contribution should inspire others to be the kind of person Albert Schweitzer had in mind when he declared: "Behind every distinguished man or woman there usually stands at least one great teacher."

Donald A. Vetter
Director for Christian Day Schools
The American Lutheran Church

Preface

Without the help of the children who have passed through my classroom doors this book could not have been written. They have come (and gone) one year after another, those eager to learn, those not eager to learn, and those with show-me attitudes. There have been children with extremely high intelligence quotients, and those with low. There have been carefree children, and many with troubled minds. I have taught, or in moments of despair, hoped and prayed I have taught.

In selections involving children and others, names have been changed, situations have been altered to protect the privacy of those concerned. However, the problems and their solutions remain true to the actual happenings. The chapters coordinate with the weeks and seasons of the school year.

The years have been, and are, good years. The children, I often believe, have taught me as much as I have taught them. But through these years, I know God has been with me, helping me all the way, using His Son, the Master teacher as an example. My gratitude runs deep. My debt to all who have come my way can never be repaid.

I acknowledge, with appreciation to the following, for permissions to use many of the selections in this book: David C. Cook Publishing Company, Light and Life Press, Augsburg Publishing House, American Sunday School Union, The Sunday School Board of Southern Baptist Convention, Mennonite Publishing House, Concordia Publishing House. In some cases, the articles have been slightly altered to suit the purposes of this book.

My special thanks to my 'sister' Mabel Montgomery, Jane Matthey, Melaine Timko and Kathie Lorei for their contributions to the prayers of this book. Thanks, too, to

Frankie Wise, Donna Pringle, Maxine Cody and Helen Weber.

To Donald Vetter, for his many inspirations, thanks. I am deeply grateful to Norma C. Camp, my editor, who patiently and expertly led me through the final preparations of the manuscript. And to Ray Puechner, my agent, a special thanks for his encouragement and loving concern.

Mary A. Vandermey

Fall Inspirations

1—A Prayerful Pause
In September's Doorway

Psalm 32:8: *"I will instruct thee and teach thee in the way which thou shalt go: I will guide thee with mine eye."*
Mark 6:34: *"And Jesus, when he came out, saw much people, and was moved with compassion toward them, because they were as sheep not having a shepherd: and he began to teach them many things."*
Psalm 121:1, 2: *"I will lift up mine eyes unto the hills, from whence cometh my help. My help cometh from the Lord, which made heaven and earth."*

I arrived early, long before the other teachers that first day of school. The playgrounds were silent, waiting. The empty swings swayed in the autumn breeze. The buses had not yet begun to spill their cargoes of laughing children onto the campus.

I walked to my room. *My* room. It was new to me for this was to be my first year at the Christian school. My mind was full of plans, but I was reluctant to think of them now. I am given to flights of fancy, even to poetry, but I am also practical, for I am a teacher.

As I inserted my key into the lock I hesitated. For this moment I permitted the fanciful to take possession of me. September is a special month. The air is heavy with the rich ripe smells of harvest time. The mountains to the north are dry, yellowed from the heat of the long hot desert summer. A haze obscures the peaks. It is harvest time; the growing season has passed. But for the teacher, September is planting time.

I put aside the poetic and gathered my practical self together and turned the key.

The sharp smell of soap and wax filled the room. I stood beside my desk. *My* desk. I am grateful I did not know for how many years it was to be my daytime home. My courage might have failed me. But the not knowing protected me.

I scanned the room. The floors shined with wax. Soon they would be scuffed by scores of little shoe treads. The desks were lined up in neat rows. Soon they would be pushed this way and that by restless children. The bulletin boards were bright with the results of my artistic endeavors of the previous week. There were illustrated Bible lessons, science lessons. Readers, arithmetic books, Bible study books, supplies of paper waited on the shelves.

The room's silence was loud in my ears. Soon the desks would be crowded with class members. The children's minds would be crowded with questions. What would Teacher be like? The idea of the probing disconcerted me. Would I be able to live up to their expectations of me? Be a good teacher? I mentally scanned my ambitions for those children, and for myself.

I looked through the shining windows to the great dusty mountains. No matter what the weather, in sunshine or rain, I know they are there. Just as no matter what comes, I know God *is*. In this moment of uncertainty, I faced the mountains. Symbolically, I faced God. I realized He knows my weaknesses, my strengths. I placed myself, my hopes, my plans before Him.

"Lord, I will try earnestly, prayerfully to walk as Jesus walked. I will try to follow the teaching of the Master.

"Each day I will endeavor to leave my personal concerns at home. They have no place in the schoolroom.

"I will take time to listen to each child's story, aware that to the child his story is important."

Pausing in my prayer, I watched a lazy cloud drift across a peak, then float to the other side of the range.

I continued my prayer. "I will not permit my intense desire for accomplishment to make me impatient with the laggard. Instead I will try to learn the reason for his lack of accomplishment, and work from there.

"Lord, help me remember the child's importance to himself as an individual. He must feel needed in the class.

"Give me ideas that will make studies, academic and Bible, exciting learning experiences for the children."

The sounds of the first buses arriving, the shouts of eager children momentarily interrupted my meditation. Determinedly I closed my mind to the sounds and continued my solitary prayer.

"Each day too, I will take a fragment of time for myself, to refill from Your Word, O Lord, the well of me which will be so rapidly emptied into the classroom. I will pause to appreciate the beauties of Your world—clouds, mountains, stars, Your people. I will take time to listen to music which stirs me. I will take time for Bible reading, for prayer, for communion with You.

"And having recharged myself, I will remember I am Teacher. That the children will be a reflection of me.

"This is a large order, Lord. My favorite poet, Robert Browning, said, 'A man's reach should exceed his grasp, or what's a heaven for.' I place these requests, these ambitions before You now. I know You will be with me throughout this year."

So I aspired, I planned, I prayed in faith.

The door opened. The children began arriving. Noise filled the room. I knew my school year had begun.

Heavenly Father,

Help me to use my hands gently as Jesus did.

Help me to use my voice as I believe He would want it used. Help me to use my mind and heart as though they were reflections of Him.

Help me to remember love means giving of myself, not part, but all, remembering Jesus gave all for me.

For Your guidance, Dear God, I am grateful. Amen.

2—What Shall I Do With Jerry?

Hebrews 6:15: *"And so, after he had patiently endured, he obtained the promise."*
Hebrews 10:36: *"For ye have need of patience, that, after ye have done the will of God, ye may receive the promise."*
Luke 8:15: *"But that on the good ground are they, which in an honest and good heart, having heard the word, keep it, and bring forth fruit with patience."*

What shall I do with Jerry? I asked myself a week after school year opened. He was chubby, round-faced. He was hyper-kinetic, with an IQ in the 140s. Early, Jerry became the one troublesome element in the room of third graders.

He refused to add or subtract two-digit numbers. Nevertheless, he brought me pages of four-digit numbers added correctly. I praised him for solving the difficult problems, then explained he must do the simple ones too.

When we learned multiplication tables, he promptly forgot the assignments, but brought to my desk a problem with numbers into trillions which he had multiplied by eight. What did it matter that he had worked from left to right?

It was my custom to give weekly awards of bright-colored pieces of construction paper decorated with stars, blue ribbons or pictures I had drawn. The children who received these awards were those who obeyed classroom rules, faithfully completed assignments, and acted as good Christians do. In an attempt to encourage Jerry, I gave him one though it was questionable whether he really deserved it.

He flung it on the floor. "It's only an old piece of paper!"

"Jerry!" the children protested, "Mrs. Vandermey made them especially for us!"

"Shish!" he retorted, using his favorite word of disgust.

Hoping to impress him, I withheld the awards from him for several weeks. Eventually he actually earned awards. His mother reported he was making a poster of them for his room.

But he continually interrupted with questions. "How big is the moon? How big is the sun? How hot is it? How many miles around the sun?" I took refuge in the encyclopedia. "Some teacher!" he commented and I promptly placed him in the hot seat, a desk beside mine, to contemplate his words.

In the reading group (he was in A-1) he seemed to listen with an inner ear, for unless I watched, he invariably had a volume of nature studies I kept for my own use, placed on top of his reader. Result—hot seat again.

I did much praying over Jerry, asking God for guidance. The answer took some time. Finally, His answer came through my doctor-friend. He gave me a clearer understanding of Jerry.

He said, "Hyper-kinetic children can't tune out extraneous stimuli as they react to everything. I liken them to high-powered autos in need of a tune-up. They've got the horsepower, but not the performance. The basic cause seems to be physical which includes the brain. . . . Many hyper-kinetics have high IQs. We now have medication to partially control it. It's paradoxical that a depressant to slow down an overactive child normally, may cause this type of child to be even more overactive.

"So we use the reverse type of medication. One sure thing is that it buys time for the child. If he can be slowed down, he will be more in step with his peers as he nears puberty."

I need patience, I realized. "God, grant me patience," I prayed, "more, more patience!"

Soon Jerry developed a tic. I told his mother what the doctor had said and her pediatrician ordered the medication. I was to give Jerry the pill noontimes. The tic continued. I discovered he had been hiding the pill in his mouth, then spitting it out later.

I tried joking with him. I tried treating him on a person-to-person level rather than teacher-student. But he took advantage of me. Result—the principal's office to contemplate his misdeeds.

I tried interesting him in playground activities. "Shish!" he replied. To prove his point, he sat on the swing, his mind no doubt busy with some astronomical problem. I loved him dearly. My non-conformist!

I tried to teach him cursive writing. "That's wrong!" he objected. Result: more prayers on my part for Jerry and for me.

Soon a two-part series of articles on the hyper-kinetic child appeared in our daily paper. A well-known pediatrician explained the problem in detail. His diagnosis, his recommended treatment, was the same as that of my doctor-friend.

The second of the series concerned a "Mrs. White," mother of a hyper-kinetic boy, and her problems. It explained how they tried to treat him as an adult in a child's body, and how they kept tools and lumber for his use. They also kept progress charts.

The last of the article depressed me. The mother related her son's school experience in the past year. "We enrolled our son in a Christian school. For the first time we see progress. He has an understanding teacher. She is strict, yet she knows our son, she handles him with kindness. He is better behaved. I wish this teacher could go with him all through school. . . ."

Where had I failed Jerry? Surely God hadn't failed me!

I determined to learn the identity of that teacher and learn her secret.

When Jerry's mother came for spring conference I was dismayed to see she brought the articles I'd read.

"Did you see these articles in the paper?" she asked. I said I had.

"Do you know who that teacher is?"

I said no, but I wished I did. Was she going to tell me I'd failed with Jerry?

"That teacher is you. That mother, Mrs. White, is me. I thank you and God too, for all you've done for Jerry. He needed someone to be patient with him, to humor him, to take time, to be kind. You were all that. You've helped his father and me too. . . ." She dabbed at sudden tears.

My prayers for God's help and guidance had paid off. He

had wanted to teach me patience. That had taken longer than I'd wanted it to take.

What had I really done for Jerry? I wondered. I had tried to adjust to each turn he made in the classroom. I had tried to answer his questions as adult to adult. I had humored him. I had punished him when he needed punishment. Right then and there, in silence, I thanked God for His patience with me, for His gentle touch on my mind.

Heavenly Father,

As teachers, let us ever be aware of the special needs of each child in our care. Teach us patience. Give us fortitude in searching out the potential within each child.

Remind us we cannot wait for hidden ability to appear. We must work to uncover it. And having uncovered it, may we have the wisdom to feed it so that each child may increase in knowledge and wisdom.

For all the blessings You have so freely given us, thank You. Amen.

3—The Impossible Boy*

John 5:30: *"I can of mine own self do nothing: as I hear, I judge: and my judgment is just; because I seek not mine own will, but the will of the Father which hath sent me."*
Romans 14:13: *"Let us not therefore judge one another any more: but judge this rather, that no man put a stumblingblock or an occasion to fall in his brother's way."*

Mrs. Richmond, fifth grade teacher, hoped she was hiding her dismay caused by Timmy Othro's enrollment in her room at the Christian day school. His reputation, both here in former years, and in public school, had preceded him. He was now in a back seat, grinning impishly as if to say, "Just wait. I haven't changed."

Preparing the morning's Bible lesson, she gave him an appraising look. He was still too thin; he still had that thrown-together look. She knew his parents were separated and neither wanted him. He lived with a married sister.

He saw the glance and flashed back a confident smile, plainly saying, "I'm ready! Dare you to change me!"

She opened the Bible to Romans 5:8 and read, "But God commendeth his love toward us, in that, while we were yet sinners, Christ died for us.

"Let's think about it, Class. How does God show His love for us?"

"We are saved through Jesus who died for us," Deb replied.

"Jesus is God's only Son. He gave up someone He loved for us. That sure proves a lot."

Joe said, "I've asked forgiveness. I ain't—I'm not sure."

Frowning, Timmy thrust long fingers through his blonde hair. "I dunno. Everybody keeps telling me I'm no good. So I go from one bad thing to another. It gets worse. I don't know why I want to be like I am, but that's me. I guess I'm the world's worst."

At least he had acquired a degree of honesty about himself, Mrs. Richmond thought, sympathizing with him.

Deb said, "You haven't killed anybody, Tim. That's an awful sin."

"Course I ain't killed nobody!"

Mrs. Richmond held up a large sheet of white paper. On it she had drawn a circle, then a line down the center. One half of the circle was unmarked. The other was filled with scraggly lines of various colors. The clean half was marked "purity," the other, "sinfulness." She explained, "These lines stand for sins. They are different in size and color. Let's name some. I'll list them on the chalkboard."

When the class had finished, the list was long: stealing; lying; talking back; cheating; fighting; hurting others.

They discussed each one: how to avoid fighting, hurting people. Answers varied, but the children concluded all must try to please the Heavenly Father because He loves us.

The premonition of trouble with Timmy still troubled Mrs. Richmond. Occasionally she wondered if the expectancy brought on his misdeeds. Her mental logbook on him read something like this:

Monday: in a scuffle over a kickball, Timmy bloodied George's nose. "But it was my ball!" yelled George. "I wanted it. I took it!" Timmy said. Confiscated the ball. After private talk with George and Tim separately they apologized to each other. Really wanted to punish Timmy, but a silent prayer (Lord, he needs my patience, my understanding) kept me from it. Tuesday: Discovered Timmy had more pencils than he should. Some children reported theirs missing. Chorus of outraged cries. "I have my initials cut in mine! I know Timmy's got it!" Said, "Timmy will let you see the pencils. If one is yours he'll return it." (Prayer: Judge righteous judgment.) Three pencils found their owners. One belonged to culprit. Timmy protested, "I found them. Finders keepers." Wednesday: Timmy would not do homework. Kept him in recess to supervise. He did work—partly. Praised him for efforts.

Mrs. Richmond called the sister in for a conference. She was defensive, antagonistic. "He doesn't cause *me* trouble. If you know how to handle him, he's all right."

Expert at concealing dismay, Mrs. Richmond replied, "I'll do the best I can." (More patience, please, Lord.)

Next an irate gas station owner across the street from the school visited. "A kid from here stole pliers and a screwdriver from me!"

"Did you see the child?" The teacher struggled for calmness.

"Tall, thin, long blond hair." The man's hands knotted together as if he were already squeezing the boy's neck.

Timmy. "I'll investigate, Mr. Madison."

She called Timmy in. (More, more patience, please!) "Timmy, Mr. Madison complained some tools are missing from his shop. Will you help me search the desks? Perhaps someone just happened to see them and carelessly brought them here."

His mouth turned hard. But together, she moving cautiously, he, reluctantly, they searched until they reached his desk. She waited for him to lift the top. It took some time. Inside, under a rat's nest of papers, they found the tools.

"Timmy, what did we learn about stealing?"

"It's a sin."

"Right."

"Timmy, I want you to return the tools to Mr. Madison. Tell him you're sorry. I want you to ask God to forgive you. I'm sure Mr. Madison will forgive you. But I'm going to ask something of you, that you do your best to be the Christian I know you can be. Obey school rules. Study harder. Earn the right to go on to sixth next year." She really wanted to spank him.

He looked past her, out the window. When he turned back, his eyes were tear-filled. "I promise, Mrs. Richmond. But I ain't going to make it. It's too late."

She put an arm across his shaking shoulder. "It's never too late, Timmy. Let Jesus come into your heart. We know if we're sorry for our mistakes, and ask forgiveness, God always forgives. We can begin again." She felt a surge of love for him.

Timmy did try. She watched him struggle with himself. Failing, succeeding—well, part of the time.

Final report card time came. Would he pass? She averaged and reaveraged his grades. He had tried. She decided he had earned promotion.

Last day of school came. All the desks were cleared of personal belongings. With cries of good-byes, and "Thanks for the good report card, Mrs. Richmond!" the children rushed off. All except Timmy.

Alone at his desk, his head was down, his body was shaking. She went to him, put her arm on his shoulder. "Timmy, what is wrong?"

He looked up. Tears were on his face. "Why did you pass me? I want to be with you. You're the only one who's ever been good to me!"

No child had ever cried over promotion from her room before. "Timmy, you've worked hard. You earned it. We must all move on."

He thought it over. "I guess . . . you're right." He rose, gathered together his notebooks. "I'll miss you." He flung his arms around her, grew self-conscious, then ran.

She did not hear from him until fall. He did not return to school. One day the principal gave her a letter. It was from Timmy.

She read it in the privacy of her room. Pinned to the top of an essay was a note from Timmy:

Dear Mrs. Richmond: here is something I wrote in Religion class in this school I am at. Thank you for helping me. Timmy. P.S. I'm glad you passed me.

The essay was titled, "My Heart is God's Home."

My heart is Christ's home because He loves me and He is my Saviour. If I let Christ into my heart, I know He takes care of me. I might have sinned a lot of times, but I try to do my best everyday. I sometimes feel mean and kick Christ out of my heart, but He forgives me when I'm sorry. Then I try harder. I do this because I had a teacher who liked me and always understood. Like Jesus always understands. My teacher's name was Mrs. Richmond.

Near tears, Mrs. Richmond placed the letter in her Bible.

Sometimes, she thought, you try and try and believe you've failed. Sometimes you never know whether you've failed or succeeded. "Thank you, Lord, for letting me know."

She thought of Timmy. The impossible boy, who through God's help, was becoming a boy with possibilities.

Dear Lord,

Thank You for the Timmies of our lives, the Timmies who test our patience, our faith.

Thank You for the strength to use in efforts to help troubled children.

Thank You for Your nearness when we call for help.

Thank You for placing us where we can serve You through others. In surrendering our lives to You, we find fulfillment. Amen.

4—Do They Know How To Pray?*

Luke 11:1: *"And it came to pass, that, as he was praying in a certain place, when he ceased, one of his disciples said unto him, Lord, teach us to pray, as John also taught his disciples."*
I Timothy 2:1: *"I exhort therefore, that first of all, supplications, prayers, intercessions, and giving of thanks, be made for all men."*
James 5:16: *"Confess your faults one to another, and pray one for another, that ye may be healed. The effectual fervent prayer of the righteous man availeth much."*

For several weeks after beginning the year teaching third grade, I felt increasing dissatisfaction at prayertime. The children seemed to be praying simply because it was expected of them. We closed our morning Bible study with the Lord's Prayer. We said grace noontimes. We said a memorized prayer before leaving for home.

I was moved to action when a new student in repeating the Lord's Prayer, said, "Our Father who art in heaven, *Hollowed out* be thy name," and not one child noticed the error.

So one day we talked about the meaning of our Master's prayer. We discussed what 'Our Father' means—that God is our heavenly Father, watching over us, just as our earthly fathers do. And on through the prayer we went.

Later, instead of the usual repetition of the Lord's Prayer, I asked for particular things we should and could pray about.

The suggestions came fast once the idea had been put into minds.

From the list of suggestions we finally settled on a prayer schedule for the week: Mondays—thankfulness; Tuesdays—our families; Wednesdays—others (including the world); Thursdays—the sick; Fridays—ourselves. We would also have a short silent prayer each day to pray about those things we want to keep to ourselves.

The first day, extrovert Joe was prayer leader. But there he stood, teetering on uneasy feet, tugging at his red sweater. Finally he folded his hands, closed his eyes. Nothing happened. He turned to me, his eyes wide and fearful. "Mrs. Vandermey, I guess I don't know how to pray. I mean out of my heart."

Corrinne spoke up. "We never pray at our house except at bedtime. Everybody's too busy with Mom working and all of us getting ready to leave. Where's the time to come from?"

I explained to Joe that before we say prayers of thankfulness, perhaps we should know what we are thankful for. The children waved their hands like flags in a breeze.

"Thank you for ourselves," Dan, a brain-damaged child said.

This needed clarification. "What do you mean, Dan?"

After a pause he said, "I don't know . . . Maybe I just mean I'm glad I'm me and can go to school."

Frances said, "I think he's glad God brought him into this world so he could enjoy God's world."

Another child added, "Thank you for protecting my father when he had to get up on the roof to fix the TV antenna."

"Thank you for us little guys. Thank you for a purpose in life," said Bob.

"What do you mean?" asked Debra who always went for the whys.

"I want my mother and father to be proud of me. Not ashamed I was born. Take Mrs. Adkins, next door to us. Her George went and got himself in jail, and she wishes all the time she'd never had him."

Another child said, "I think a purpose in life is to tell others how happy it is when you're a Christian."

Joe, by now, had recovered his composure and repeated the expressions of thankfulness the children had made.

Then came silent prayer. All heads bowed, all hands

folded. Silence came softly, reverently as we approached our Father. Each child prayed from his own innermost self.

Later in the week, the class prayed for others—our president, that the "big bomb" wouldn't drop on the world, for the wild animals caught in forest fires.

Parents became involved. They sent messages asking the children to pray for sick relatives. Children prayed for themselves—that they'd not be afraid at test time.

We went through almost an entire pregnancy of the mother of one class member, as Steven prayed on successive weeks. "Help my mother get over being sick mornings so the baby she's going to have won't be lost. . . . Please help my mother's baby be strong and healthy. . . . Please help my mother's baby to come soon. . . . Thank You, my mother's baby came and it's healthy and has two arms and two legs . . . Thank You for my new brother."

One prayer for others was particularly touching. The children knew I was privately tutoring a mentally retarded girl, and one child asked, "Please, God, help Mrs. Vandermey to give Jeri a brain she can use."

Dear God, I thought, it's impossible! But if I, the leader of these earnest children, felt disbelief, how could I expect positive results? I took heart, remembering all things are possible according to God's will. I couldn't give Jeri a new brain, but I could help her to use what she had.

As we progressed through the weekly schedule, we did have upsets. "Teacher," Joe yelled one morning, "Ramona's not praying. She had her eyes open!"

Ramona fired back, "I was so too. I guess God can hear you even if you have your eyes open while you pray. Anyway, you mustn't have been praying very hard if you were watching me! God wants us to mind our own business. Grandma says that!"

It was rewarding as well as revealing, this teaching children to really pray. One day a mother visited me. "David told me about your prayer schedule. He asked if we could do it at home too . . . He says it makes you feel good. You begin thinking of someone beside yourself."

As the year ended, I saw eight-year-olds praying aloud before others in simple, confident, unassuming ways, thinking of others, asking definite help for themselves. Being thankful. They were forming a habit-pattern to help them in their prayer lives as they progressed through school. Praying not just because it was the thing to do, but making their words meaningful segments of their lives.

Heavenly Father,

As workers with children, may we always have the teaching Spirit of Your Son. May we too learn as we teach.

Each day we ask You to guide us.

May we leave the imprint of Your infinite mind on the children in our care so they may grow in Christian love and deeds throughout their lives. Amen.

5—Keep Our Pads Peaceful

Isaiah 26:3: *"Thou wilt keep him in perfect peace, whose mind is stayed on thee: because he trusteth in thee."*
Psalm 122:7: *"Peace be within thy walls, and prosperity within thy palaces."*
II Corinthians 13:11: *"Finally, brethren, farewell. Be perfect, be of good comfort, be of one mind, live in peace; and the God of love and peace shall be with you."*

The day was off to a bad start. Even before the morning bell rang one of my third grade boys had pushed another, giving him a skinned knee. Two girls had quarreled over the use of a swing. In contrast to the usual order and quiet as they entered the room, the children were noisy.

I asked for quiet, but it was a long time coming. We began lessons. Clearly though, the children's minds were upset. "Class," I said, "we can't study when there is noise."

Joe raised his hand. "I want to ask something first. It ain't—I mean isn't—about lessons. Why does God let all the trouble happen in the world?" His face was creased with worry.

"What do you mean, Joe?"

"This morning Dad watched the news. There was fighting everywhere. And a man down our street had to go to the hospital."

"Yeah," Tom added. "I think about it too."

Now thirty faces turned to me, begging answers. What to reply? Could these children understand a solution that worked for me when I asked myself those same questions?

But present-day children are perceptive, I knew. Our rapid communications systems expose them to the entire world each day. "We don't know why God lets bad things happen. But shall I tell you a secret I have?"

Now the faces were eager. I must somehow make real positive contact with them. "After we've had a bad day here, do you think your teacher goes home feeling peaceful?"

Judy replied, "I guess not. Like yesterday when you had to send Linda and me to the office for being selfish and not letting the others have the swing."

Testing my thoughts, I began. "I have what I call a peaceful island. When I start home after school, I tell myself that if anyone has hurt my feelings, I'll say, 'Bless him, God' about that person. I just say to myself, I've done all I could to make the day a happy one. Now I'm going home to my peaceful island. I go to my house, turn on the radio to the station broadcasting peaceful music. My cat, Brother Smith—you know about him—comes in, jumps on my lap and purrs because I'm home with him. And I pray every day.

"Sometimes when I feel upset anyway, I say Psalm 23, 'The Lord is my shepherd . . .' "

As I spoke the familiar words, the children recited with me. When we finished, they began to reveal home events.

"My mom goes out for a walk by herself sometimes," Sandra said. "When she leaves, she's always nervous. When she comes back, she's smiling. I guess she's been sitting on her peaceful island."

Paul added, "My dad and mom go walking together even when it's raining. Now I know why."

Another child, obviously troubled, added, "I'm going to tell my mom and dad about this. Maybe if they could find a peaceful island, they'd not fight so much."

Germaine had been drawing and now brought a picture to show. From our art lessons she had chosen the cartoon cats, standing on hind legs, paws together, making the peace sign. The circled words indicating one cat's speech read, "Keep our pads peaceful."

Delighted, I showed the picture to the class. Immediately the other children began drawing, writing furiously. They drew stick figures, wrote sentences. "My eyeland of peace . . ." "my island of piece. . . ." I refrained from correcting spelling. The idea was important.

Joe had a map of the world. He had drawn circles all over it. Some with hands connecting them. "This is the way it ought to be all over the world. Islands of peace. All of them touching. Everybody thinking good thoughts."

"How can we help right here?" I asked.

"We can say please . . . thank you. . . . We can stop fighting. . . . We can share. . . . We can obey our parents. . . . We can obey you, Teacher. . . . We can have peaceful thoughts." It was a chorus.

Keith now approached my desk. "Teacher, I'd like some tape. I want to stick my island-of-peace sign to my desk so I can see it all the time and where the rest of you can see it too."

I produced the tape and suddenly everyone wanted his motto taped to his desk. That done, we began the neglected math.

Now a small hand directly in front of me waved urgently. Deanna, the smallest, most immature child asked, "Mrs. Vandermey, couldn't you write an article about this? Maybe our islands of peace idea would help others if they knew about it."

Surprised at her perception, I replied, "Why, I know I can, Deanna."

So now, I have written it.

Dear Lord,

In whom we find our daily strength, let me hear Your voice today.

Let me be of peaceful mind so that I may help others to be peaceful and happy.

Let me be more appreciative of the good. Let me be less contrary, wanting my way. Let my ways always be Your ways.

When the day has ended, let me have the peace that passes all understanding—the grateful knowledge You have been with me this day. Amen.

6—Dinner Of Rocks*

Proverbs 7:6, 7: *"For at the window of my house I looked through my casement, and beheld among the simple ones, I discerned...a young man void of understanding."*
Luke 6:45: *"A good man out of the good treasure of his heart bringeth forth that which is good . . . for of the abundance of the heart his mouth speaketh."*
Luke 12:34: *"For where your treasure is, there will your heart be also."*

Two months of the Christian elementary school year had passed and to the teacher, eight-year-old George remained as undisciplined and irritating as he had at the beginning. His attention span was limited to the few seconds required to open a book. From then on, his eyes wandered to the window, and he studied the mountains in the distance. What was he dreaming of, what was he searching for in those high places?

His attention next shot to the girl passing his desk. Inevitably his foot shot out to trip her. Result—howls of protest from the victim. Further result—punishment for the culprit, who cried, "Nobody likes me!"

The problem continued. When George did look at his reader, he lost his place and someone had to point it out to him. He could not—or would not—read anyway. The teacher despaired even while she prayed for a way to solve the George-problem.

* From *Evangel*, October 1969, as "God's Windows," by permission of Light and Life Press.

She read her Bible, searching for inspiration. She came upon Matthew 7:7: "Ask, and it shall be given you; seek, and ye shall find; knock, and it shall be opened unto you."

Well, the teacher mused later, most always what we ask for and what we receive aren't exactly what we think we've asked for. We knock and we are invited into a room completely different from what we pictured. We want the Georges and the Tammys to be automatically receptive to what we must teach. But God has made these children walk a different path.

One day at recess time, the teacher saw George in a far corner of the playground. Squatting in the sand, his plaid shirt hanging over drooping jeans, he looked like a gnome. His busy hands were making the sand fly. With a smile, the teacher approached him.

"What are you looking for, George?"

"Nothin'," he replied, quickly heaping the sand to hide some object.

"I thought I saw a pretty red rock here the other day." The teacher was entering the strange room after knocking as the Bible had said.

"Wasn't red. It's green quartz." George began to dig like a frantic gopher, spattering sand over his teacher's shoes.

Dark eyes shining, triumphant, the child tugged the shining glass-like rock from its earthy bed. Spitting on it and rubbing it against his sleeve, then holding it up for admiration, he said, "Look! Pretty! Kin I have it for my collection? I've got thousands. Agates, tourmalines, geodes, and . . ."

Why, the teacher thought, George just can't be interested in everyday stories when he knows so much about these things. No wonder he's bored.

"George, I have a friend who collects rocks," the teacher said. "She has what she calls a dinner of rocks. She's hunted until she has rocks that look like fried eggs, loaves of bread and even baked ham!"

"She does? I wish she were my mom. My mom is so sick of hearing me explain them to her, she won't listen . . . Teacher, do you know how this rock got this way? It's . . ."

"Would you like to show the class your rock collection for science next week and explain the types to the class?"

He stood up. He seemed much taller. "Would I?"

George presented his rocks to the class. He even asked

Joan, the girl who sat next to him, to help. And he told of his teacher's friend with the dinner of rocks. "Someday I'm going to have one of those collections!" he added. And then gathered his rocks together and sat down.

George set no scholastic records that year. But with the recognition of his worth as a rock-expert, he took more interest in his work. "After all," he said, "if I'm gonna be an expert, I have to know how to learn from books as well as from the dirt."

That night the teacher prayed earnestly and gratefully. Earnestly, that she might never be remiss in finding a child's potential; gratefully, that God had permitted her to enter George's private room and so discover the treasure there.

Heavenly Father,

As a teacher let me ever be alert in discovering the potential of each child. Teach me to be ready to appreciate what treasure is in the mental room of each child.

Remind me I cannot wait. I must work to discover before it is too late for me to help. And having discovered, may I have the wisdom to polish, so that another child may learn to serve You better. Amen.

7—To Blast Or To Bless

Psalm 1:1: "Blessed is the man that walketh not in the counsel of the ungodly nor standeth in the way of sinners, nor sitteth in the seat of the scornful."

Matthew 5:44: "But I say unto you, Love your enemies, bless them that curse you, do good to them that hate you, and pray for them that despitefully use you, and persecute you."

Romans 2:20: "*An instructor of the foolish, a teacher of babes,* which hast the form of knowledge and of the truth in the law."

The teacher was disturbed. Janie, a new girl in the class, was insecure, self-defensive and disruptive. The teacher ran out of negatives in thinking about her, and in trying to help her adjust to this strange situation, began to think in positive ways. The mother had enrolled Janie in this Christian school, hoping the environment would help. But would it?

Constantly the child rushed into the classroom during recess. "I'll show them someday! Nobody can push me around!"

"Janie, I'm surprised," the teacher said, comfortingly. "You want to make friends here, don't you?"

"I don't know. Everybody everywhere just hates me! I wish I didn't have to go to school. I hate it. Everybody picks on me. I'll get even!"

What could cause her to be so strongly on the defensive? "You heard your Sunday school teacher say we should turn the other cheek. What does that mean?"

"It means let everybody run over me. They can't do that to me. My father says never let that happen!"

She was in no mood for advice, or counsel, so the teacher asked Janie to help her straighten the books on the reading table. Momentarily, she quieted, but the outrages at the unfairness Janie felt she had suffered, continued. "Clarice won't let me play with her and her friends. So I took her puzzle book! I was just looking at it. I didn't mean to tear a page!"

"Didn't you, Janie?" the teacher asked without accusation.

Janie looked out the window, not answering.

The teacher tried consoling, reasoning, and then lifting her ego. "Janie, you are such a pretty girl when you smile (which was true). You're good at reading and writing. If you'd try, really try to make friends, you could. Try to be more understanding. Try to make the children like you by being kind." The teacher felt she sounded like a stuck PA system.

The next time Janie rushed into the room, tears streaking her face, the teacher first heard her out. "Mrs. Gaines (the principal) bawled me out for taking off my shoes and walking in the dirt in my socks. They're my socks! I'm going to leave this school!"

"Janie, were you in church when the minister said the benediction? He said 'May the Lord bless you and keep you.' If we ask the Lord's blessing we should bless others, then we'll feel good toward others and can forgive them if they hurt us. Why not try blessing those who hurt you, Janie? Maybe you'd feel better toward them. You wouldn't be wishing bad to come to them. You'd like them better because we can't dislike those we bless. It is like God blessing us because He loves us.

"Why don't you look up the word 'bless' in the dictionary, then try to do as it says? Here."

The girl just stared at the dictionary placed before her. Slowly, she began paging through it while the teacher corrected papers.

"Teacher," Janie finally exclaimed, "you're wrong about that bless word. The word means . . . I'll read it. It says right here, 'To blow up with an explosive.' That's what everybody needs!"

The teacher felt a chill, but looked at the place where the child pointed in the page. "Janie, you found the word 'blast'. . . ." The teacher and child laughed together.

"Here it is—bless—'to pray for the happiness of someone.'"

"How can I pray for the happiness of those kids that pick on me?" Belligerence stuck out all over the child.

"You don't have to say it aloud. Just to yourself."

"I can't."

"Say it."

"Teacher," she whined. But she smiled then jumped up and ran outside. Had Janie been reached finally?

Two weeks passed. There were the usual cries of mistreatment. Each time the teacher comforted and let Janie go.

But one day she came into the classroom grinning. "Teacher, I guess you're right about the blessing business. Out there I said if I couldn't lead the class in 'First in, Last out' I'd not play. Course they wouldn't let me. I walked away. And Teacher, I tried, I really tried. I kept saying bless you, bless you as I walked away. I didn't look back. I kept saying the words so hard, look what I did." She held out her hands, palms up.

There were deep marks, stained red, where her nails had cut in.

"I finally went back. I said I'd take my turn. I was still mad because I didn't have my way. But they said I could play. I did. Nobody seemed to hate me anymore. I felt a little better. They let me play. I guess maybe you're right about the blessing-business. I just have to keep at it if I'm going to be happy."

Janie was on her way.

Dear Lord,

When hurt feelings, when quarrels disturb our rooms, help us to find ways to bring peace where there seems to be no chance for peace.

Help us to strengthen characters, even temperaments, in the children so that when they become adults they will be creators of harmony; friends instead of enemies; instruments of peace where there seems to be no hope of peace.

For Your guidance through the Word, we do give thanks always. Amen.

8—Important Words

Psalm 33:1: *"Rejoice in the Lord, O ye righteous: for praise is comely for the upright."*
Isaiah 41: 6, 7: *"They helped every one his neighbor; and every one said to his brother, Be of good courage. So the carpenter encouraged the goldsmith, and he that smootheth with the hammer."*

Mike, a shy, inhibited eight-year-old, was enrolled in third grade as a repeater from a large school. His mother hoped the shelter and Christian guidance he would receive in the smaller Christian school would help him not only emotionally but scholastically. However, the mother didn't leave all the work of building Mike's morale to the teacher. At Open House, she visited his room, talked with the teacher, and then examined the work her son had done.

Afterward, the teacher went around the room, straightening the children's papers on the desks. On Mike's desk was a note from his mother: "You're doing fine, Mike. I'm proud of you. Keep up the good work. I love you. Mother."

Another teacher noticed at lunchtime one day that Linda always smiled when she began opening her lunchbox. "Your mother must prepare extra special lunches for you everyday," the teacher said. "You're always so happy at this time." Many of the children complained they didn't like what their mothers sent.

"Oh, yes," replied Linda brightly. "But my mother always

puts a love note to me in the box. My daddy does too. When he's home, that is. I can hardly wait to see what each one says." The child quickly unfolded a bit of kitchen paper towel. "Today it says, 'I'm glad God sent you to me, Linda. Daddy says to tell you he's twice as happy as I am and that's a lot. Love, Mother.'"

Important words.

What important words could I say to my pupils? To a class, apprehensive before a test, important words might be, "Remember to think, God says, 'I am with you always.'"

"Joe, I'm proud of you. You worked every problem correctly. Next time, why don't you line up the problems as they are in the book and number them? But this is the best you've ever done."

"If you work hard alone, I'm sure you can do your work correctly. Then you may work a puzzle at the reading table."

"Judy, will you please pick up the papers in the aisle? Someone dropped them."

"Let's all clean our desks today?" (rather than, "Clean your desks. They're a disgrace.")

"Our class," (not, "my class"); "our room," (not, "my room.")

"Please. . .Thank you. . .I'm proud of you!. . .This is the best you've ever done." Important words.

Dear Lord,

Help us to teach Christian living by being examples of honesty, good judgment, forth-rightness, fair play, reverence for You.

We offer all our thoughts, words and deeds to You, knowing You will guide us in dealing with unforeseen problems and work in our school days.

May we always think of the child's value of himself. Amen.

9—Answer To A Prayer*

Mark 6:34: *"And Jesus, when he came out, saw much people, and was moved with compassion toward them, because they were as sheep not having a shepherd: and he began to teach them many things."*
Luke 9:47,48: *"And Jesus, perceiving the thought of their heart, took a child, and set him by him, and said unto them, Whosoever shall receive this child in my name receiveth me: and whosoever shall receive me receiveth him that sent me: for he that is least among you all, the same shall be great."*
Acts 20:35: *"I have shewed you all things, how that so labouring ye ought to support the weak, and to remember the words of the Lord Jesus, how he said, It is more blessed to give than to receive."*

The principal brought Mrs. Morgan and her eight-year-old Debbie into my third-grade classroom just as nine o'clock bell rang that rainy morning. After introducing me to Mrs. Morgan, she said, "And here is Debbie, joining your class!" She spoke too brightly for my comfort. I guessed: another problem child.

Struggling with my errant thoughts, I welcomed the new student. She was small, grey-eyed. In fact, she seemed a grey child. She wore a much-washed dress, her ash-brown hair straggling across her shoulders.

At the door, preparing to leave, Mrs. Morgan twisted her

---

* From *Evangel*, February 1970, by permission of Light and Life Press.

hands together. "I hope you can do something for Debbie." She faded away.

My principal later confirmed my first impression. "She has a low IQ. She failed second grade, but they decided to let her go on. Do the best you can."

It was much worse than I thought. The child didn't know her basic adds and takeaways. She read at first-grade level. During Bible class her head dropped to her desk. She sobbed. I asked why she was crying.

"I don't know about Jesus. Who was He? I don't know nothing about anything. My father never teached me!"

The father? I wondered.

The children gathered about. "We'll help you, Debbie. We always help each other here."

The crying stopped.

We began reading. Martha held the book for the stranger, even using her fingers for a liner. As Debbie read, Martha helped her sound out words.

Arithmetic was no better. I felt totally inadequate to help. Where was the time with thirty-three others? But when you really want to, you somehow squeeze it out. I found time, and worked to try to bring Debbie to her full potential.

But soon she began to beg off reading, saying she had a headache. She cried over arithmetic. There's no use, one side of my mind protested. The other said, "Don't give up."

Gradually I learned Deb's background. Her father had taken her and run away when she was three. He traveled with her, picking fruit and vegetables in the productive California valleys. Recently he'd died, and the child had been returned to her mother.

What chance had the child had? A deeper surge of desire to help filled me. I suggested Deb remain after school so I could help her catch up. "But I can't pay you," the mother said. Her hands twisted together again.

"I love Deb," I replied. "I just want to help."

So we began our after-school sessions. For awhile she resisted and cried, "I'm dumb!"

"Debbie, God knows about you and loves you."

She lifted her grey eyes in wonder. "Tell me about Him."

I found simple Bible storybooks and read first. As I went along, she became excited. "Let me read, please!"

For the first time Deb *wanted* to read. For the first time she *could* read. It was far below grade level, but what of it? I borrowed ditto arithmetic sheets from first grade. She took them home, returned them. They were correctly done. What matter the sheets were smudged with lines and erasures?

One afternoon after she had haltingly read the account of Jesus walking on water, she said in a small voice, "I'd like to come to Sunday school. Martha told me about it. Could I come, Teacher?"

"Of course!" I called Mrs. Morgan and she agreed Deb might attend.

That was the breakthrough. Her acceptance of Jesus and His teachings changed her completely. Walking, she gave the impression of floating. Speaking, she gave the impression of singing. She studied determinedly.

But could Deb's mind, that seemed to lack so much in learning capability, carry her on? Mid-year came, and she failed her tests. But she didn't cry. "I just have to work harder, and I have to pray for help," she said sturdily.

Inside myself, I said, "Thanks, God, for helping!"

All at once all seemed lost. Debbie announced her mother was to work as housekeeper in a distant city. She cried, "I have to leave you!" No one could comfort her.

The children planned a going-away party, took up a collection and bought a set of Bible books for her. We held the party after last recess.

As she left, she gave me two folded sheets of paper. "They're letters." We kissed good-bye.

I waited until the children had gone. The room seemed a sad place. Debbie wouldn't be here anymore.

I opened the first paper. It was from Deb, but it was not a letter. It was a story.

BY DEBRA

One day I went to a school and I had a nice teacher, and she was a good lady and she loved God and me a lot. She tried to help me as much as she cood and she was sad at first. She said I was God's child and that made me happy because I wondered lots of time whos child i was. Techer cried when she had to leave me. She said love God as He loves you and I will and I know I ll always have to work hard to learn. Form Debra.

The second letter, on pink stationery, was from Deb's mother. "Dear Teacher, thank you for helping Debra. Thank you for helping me. When my husband took Deb, I said there wasn't any God. But I guess He pushed me to the school where you are to show me He is. I began to pray you'd help Deb and you have and you've helped me. You are the answer to the first prayer I've said in a long time. Deb and I will never forget. She says she knows now she isn't dumb. She just has to work harder to catch up. I know God will bless you for what you did."

I put the letters away. I remembered the old story of the ancient one upon whom Jesus called, and each time the ancient turned him away. Why? Because Jesus had come in the guise of others. Jesus had visited me in the guise of Mrs. Morgan and Deb. In His concern for them, He had not let me fail them. He had wanted me for an answer to a prayer.

Almighty God,

Who is guilding us in our daily work, be near us today.

Remind us Your children are precious in Your sight.

Where we are at times impatient, discouraged in our efforts, and often overworked, we know Your mercy endures forever and You are near to us.

We thank You for the youth who come under our care. May we always work under the shelter of Your love and care and strength in Christian faith and kindness. Amen.

10—Hold Hands And See

I John 3:11: *"For this is the message that ye heard from the beginning, that we should love one another."*
Romans 12:18: *"If it be possible, as much as lieth in you, live peaceably with all men."*
I Timothy 2:2: " *. . . that we may lead a quiet and peaceable life in all godliness and honesty."*

There was constant bickering among the girls of the class. It had been true for three months, since school opened. I was troubled by it. This bickering destroyed the Christian conduct habits I so wanted to teach the students. At first, I was convinced time would solve the problem. Mentally, I excused the girls for their misdeeds, aware of the great imbalance in the class—only eight girls to seventeen boys. There simply weren't enough girls to go around so there would be a number of sets of "best" friends.

To further complicate matters, Kathie and Carla were black, the only children of their race enrolled in our school. And even they wouldn't play together.

So daily, Jennie, or Sue, or Carla, would meet me as I came to school. "Teacher, Julie and Kathie won't play with us," they would wail. "Kathie won't let us have turns jumping rope!"

At recess, planned games fell apart because, "Jennie won't be my partner!" Chaos took over while I wiped away tears from dark and light faces alike. I repeatedly was saying, "Girls, wouldn't it make *you* happy to have someone share with you?" My stock of admonitions dwindled. Somehow I must teach them to live in harmony and to help each other.

One morning, in my early devotional hour alone, I read the story of Jesus taking the hand of the daughter of Jairus and healing her with His touch. That brought to mind the account of Jesus in the crowd at Capernaum, and how He touched and healed the sick. His touch—the miracle touch.

Certainly, I had no such miracle touch, but perhaps I could use these lessons from the life of the Master in solving my problem. As I drove to school that day, I put mental finishing touches on a plan.

Debra and Carla met me at the car. They were crying. "Teacher," said Carla, tears making satiny streaks on her dark face, "Kathie and Debbie say they will never be our friends!"

"What did you do to make them not want to be friends?"

"Nothing. They just don't like us."

Instead of regular Bible study that morning, I read Matthew 8:5-10 and Luke 8:41-48 which had so impressed me. We held class discussion on the many kindnesses, the miracle works of Jesus. But the children simply could not relate themselves to Him. "After all," they objected, "He was the Son of God. He could do anything!"

"We can be kind, we can think of the other person. We can think about trying to make someone else happy," I countered.

"The other person ought to think about me too!" Kathie's brown eyes snapped. "It works both ways."

I dropped the subject in favor of a reading lesson.

At recess trouble began again. "Teacher, Kathie won't. . . ." "Teacher, Jennie told Debra she doesn't like me!" More tears. I used my ready supply of tissues.

Now was the time for action. I set the boys into a game of baseball, then gathered the girls into a tight little group.

"If it's hide and seek, I don't want it!" pouted Jennie.

"It's something new," I replied, with a hint of mystery children so love. "Now. All eyes shut and no peeking. I'm going to put each of you in a different place." I led them, each in turn, into another small circle, put each in a different place. "Join hands with the ones next to you."

Giggles replaced wails. "See if you can guess whose hands you are holding. First, name the right one. Then the left. Carla, you begin."

Of course, no one could guess. No one, that is, except Debra. "I'm holding Jennie's hand. I can tell by the ring she always wears!"

Jennie and Carla convulsed with laughter. "Wrong, Deb!"

The girls opened their eyes. "Jennie's wearing my ring today!" Carla screamed with laughter.

"But your skin feels the same—" Deb broke off in confusion.

"Did you think I had alligator skin?" Carla laughed at herself, clapping her dark hands together.

Now all the girls laughed together. No one had correctly guessed whose hands she had been holding.

I snatched at the opportunity to bring the lessons home. "Girls, when things go wrong, and you are angry with someone, hold hands and see if you can guess if you're holding the hand of the someone you're angry with. If you can have fun that way, think of how much fun you can have with your eyes open."

They were intrigued. All that day, I saw clusters of girls, eyes shut, hands clasped and guessing.

The next morning when I reached school, they rushed to meet me. "Teacher, we've been mad at each other three times already this morning, but every time it happened, we shut our eyes, held hands and we weren't mad anymore!" Jennie cried. Each girl added her share of the story.

"Do you know," said Jennie, "I can't tell the difference between Carla's hands and Kathie's hands, and Deb's and Sue's when I have my eyes shut. I know the colors are different. I guess their hearts and minds are the same too!"

"And you know," added Sue breathlessly, "you just can't stay mad when you hold hands. It makes you like the other person. She's your friend. Jesus meant that, I think."

Yes, but while they held hands, they thought more of the other person than of themselves. Once more the Scripture had given me the answer to my problem.

Father,

We're glad that Your love causes us to stretch our minds in seeking solutions to the problems of our classrooms. We thank You for Your Word, ever ready to help us. All we need to do is search for the answer.

We thank You for the privilege of being in this place, that here we may work to try to bring reflections of Your Son, in reminding others to love one another. Amen.

Winter Inspirations

11—Teacher On Wheels*

Joshua 1:9: *"Have not I commanded thee? Be strong and of a good courage; be not afraid, neither be thou dismayed: for the Lord thy God is with thee whithersoever thou goest."*
Psalm 27:14: *"Wait on the Lord: be of good courage, and he shall strengthen thine heart: wait, I say, on the Lord."*
Isaiah 44:14: *"He heweth him down cedars, and taketh the cypress and the oak, which he strengtheneth for himself among the trees of the forest: he planteth an ash, and the rain doth nourish it."*

The conductor spotted the young woman on crutches and shouted, "You can't board this train without someone to take care of you!"

Maxine Cody's uncle remonstrated and tried to help her aboard. The conductor put out his arm, barring the way. The determined Maxine said, "I'm getting on this train. I can take care of myself." Wilting under her straight look, he permitted her aboard. Swinging her body and crutches into a rhythm she'd learned with steel will, she entered the car.

Trouble for this blue-eyed girl began when she graduated from high school and was having pain. "Just growing pains," the friendly family doctor decided, but they were finally diagnosed as arthritis. She managed a summer session at college and taught Bible classes at her church, preparing herself to carry out her dream, to teach school.

* From *The Lutheran Standard*, copyright Augsburg Publishing House.

After securing enough credits she secured a teaching position in a one-room country school in Iowa. "I waded through snow up to my aching knees, being my own janitor," she says in the soft voice so characteristic of her. "By this time I was having pain in my hands too. God must have been very busy listening to my prayers that year, for I prayed constantly for strength. And I received it."

She was elected to teach in a small-town school next. But during Christmas vacation pain forced her to resign. God provided her with more strength the next year as she took additional college training and then she taught until Eastertime. "It seemed a vacation away from the delightful children did me more harm than good," she says.

Even that early in her career, she was "good medicine" for the children. A tenth grader who had years before been in an elementary school where she'd taught joined a drinking gang one night. In trouble, the first thing he said was, "Don't let Miss Cody hear about this. She'd be disappointed in me."

Maxine's aunt and uncle, believing the mild climate might help her, urged her to come to California. There she secured a position of sitter for two little boys.

Later the parents remarked, "We hired her because we felt sorry for her, and because the boys were fascinated with the story she told them at the interview. In no time we felt sorry for ourselves, ashamed of our complaints about little things. She radiated such faith in God."

But Maxine still wanted to teach school in Iowa even in the wheel chair she was now confined to. That was when she encountered the irate conductor who did not realize God was helping propel her.

In Iowa again, she taught summer Bible classes while looking for another teaching position. But the dampness of the church basement where she taught aggravated the arthritis. Now doctors gave their decision in a blue paperback report. Its complicated verbiage spelled out, "No hope of cure."

"I looked at that paper. My hands shook and I dropped it," she says. "But something touched me. It was like a gentle hand. The Lord was telling me I could begin at this point. I felt happy."

Miss Cody returned to California. Soon her mother and

father joined her and together they opened a Bible bookstore which they still operate. "But I wasn't satisfied," Maxine says. "I wanted to do more things with my mind."

The Lord put her in the right place at the right time. The Lutheran school where Maxine had been teaching Sunday school classes had a vacancy in fifth and sixth grades. She applied and the board hired her.

She has held this position for more than ten years and has missed only a few days because of illness. Her devoted father and mother take her to school each morning, helping her with the walker which is fitted with a seat.

She is a favorite with the children. As she scoots along to her classroom, she is constantly stopped by early arriving pupils who tell her of their adventures. Noon recesses are often taken up umpiring baseball games. She can call, "You're out!" like a pro.

Often she receives requests from her students by mail or phone. "Miss Cody," one boy wrote, "please pray for my mother. She's very sick."

A boy in fifth grade began to tremble and panic while facing an arithmetic test. Maxine moved down the aisle in her rubber-tired walker. Putting her arm across his shoulder, she whispered, "Let's pray together, John." They asked God to calm him, to open his mind so he could do well in the test. Maxine said, "God says, 'Fear not for I am with you.' " Soon the boy was at ease, busily working his problems.

"I never wanted to do anything but teach," Miss Cody declares. "I never dreamed though, I'd find my teaching in California. But God in His all-knowing and mysterious ways guided me to this place, shaping the events of my life so my work here became inevitable. He gave me the strength, the courage to go on, to accomplish whatever I have. I thank Him daily."

God, Heavenly Father,

First You make us weak, so that we may find strength in You. You make us weak so that we may know Your wisdom.

Thank You for the trials, the tests, that we through Your

constant companionship know victory over physical and mental handicaps. Amen.

12—Take Off The Dunce Caps*

Isaiah 49:22: *"Thus saith the Lord God, Behold, I will lift up mine hand to the Gentiles, and set up my standard to the people: and they shall bring thy sons in their arms, and thy daughters shall be carried upon their shoulders."*
I Peter 5:2: *"Feed the flock of God which is among you, taking the oversight thereof, not by constraint, but willingly; not for filthy lucre, but of a ready mind."*

A nationally known actress was scheduled to speak before the PTA one evening. Why had she requested to speak? I wondered as I found my seat among other elementary teachers. The audience rose, applauded, when the slender, vivacious star of the musical comedy playing at our civic theater entered. Her name was Joyce.

Smiling appreciatively, her slender hands on the podium, she waited for the applause to subside. "Mothers, fathers, teachers, I'm here tonight, not as an actress, but as a human being. In each city I play, I ask to speak to such people as you." Her dramatic pause was so long that the audience seemed to be holding its breath. She leaned an elbow on the podium now, cupped a hand around her chin and smiled. "Tonight is an anniversary of sorts for me. Twenty years ago I was released from a home for the mentally retarded. I was twelve years old."

A chorus of "no's" burst from the audience.

"It's true. My parents, my teachers said I was retarded because I failed, failed in school. I know now why I failed. I

* Formerly appeared in *Home Life*, May 1976, as "Do You Make Your Child Wear A Dunce Cap?" Copyright © 1976 The Sunday School Board of the Southern Baptist Convention. All rights reserved. Used by permission.

was scared. I had been brainwashed into believing I could not learn. Why? How? My brother and sister brought home baskets of honors. Teachers, parents said, 'Joyce, why aren't you smart like Tom and Jennie? They aren't dumb.' How was I to know I was merely a slow learner and completely beaten down? How desperately I needed inspiration, motivation. I didn't know that either.

"In the home, I, of course, associated with only brain damaged, or retarded children, and so I became a vegetable because I was convinced I was like them. Then when I was nearly twelve, a retired music teacher, working as a volunteer at the home, discovered I had a voice. Daily, I get down on my knees and thank God for that woman who became interested in me. . . . She was an answer to a prayer I had said daily, 'God, help me, please help me!' . . . That woman cut through miles of red tape and adopted me. My family had long ago rejected me. I finished high school in three years. Studied music. Oh, the joy of knowing I could learn! . . . and well, here I am!"

The audience rose. Applause filled the room.

Naturally, as a teacher I was stunned. How could such a thing have happened to this evidently brilliant woman? But I knew so well what was happening to many students with whom I was in contact. My classroom experiences, and my private tutoring sessions had taught me that parents—and some teachers too—do label students dumb. Unconsciously they put the dunce cap on certain children.

Mrs. K., mother of one of my second graders, asked plaintively one day, "What's wrong with my children? They're just plain dumb. Where did it come from? Their father and I both have our Master's. But our kids can't learn. I'm ashamed."

Ashamed—a key word. I had been in Mrs. K's home as tutor for her son, Mike. How often I'd heard her say, "Mike didn't do his homework as usual. He'd rather play than work." Mike grinned, then danced around his chair. Proud he was living up to his mother's image of him.

Another key word—dunce.

At one home, the grandmother drilled the child for an hour before I arrived. Anne's face was flushed, her eyes red from crying. Her frustrations were the result of force. She did poorly. She was afraid of doing wrong.

To add yet another example to this list of "what's wrong," take my friend, Trudy. "What am I going to do?" she moaned. "Karen has been labeled EMR (educable mentally retarded). I've had her in five schools, yet she doesn't learn. I get up tight when I try with her. It's hopeless."

Another key word—hopeless.

Dr. R.D. Laing, British psychologist, says the best way to manipulate a person is not to tell him what to do, or not to tell him what is wrong with him. Telling makes him hostile. These are examples of that kind of operation.

In my classroom, I shudder when IQ test time arrives. Not because of the work and time involved, but because I know how many of the slow students have been pressured. "Now you work hard. Get a high score or else."

My problem, as a teacher (the same applies to parents), is to try to cut the child loose from the repressed feelings—to try to heal the trauma—the what's-the-use attitudes. I tell the child, "God is with you. . . . God helps you when you ask Him. He gave you your mind to use." Once the child realizes he can learn, it's like witnessing the birth of a star. His "I getcha, Teacher!" and the triumphant smile is worth all the patience, the bolstering of the sagging ego.

What specifically can we teachers do to accomplish this "birth of a star"?

As a first step, we can search for the hidden fear in the child. Fears prevent him from relaxing so that learning can take place. Is he afraid of God's wrath? Of his teacher? Is he afraid of his parents? Of punishment? Or of being made fun of.

Second, we can give him encouragement. Not in honeyed words—he'll see through that. Tell him, "Everybody makes mistakes. That's why they put erasers on pencils." He can laugh at that. He will know he is not alone. Tell him, "I was no brain in school. I had to work hard. Because I studied hard, I didn't forget what I learned."

In my classroom and in private tutoring sessions, I use my miracle machine—a cassette recorder. Angie, an eleven-year-old, reading at second-grade level, was fascinated by the machine. We would first read and re-read a paragraph or two from her reader, or a humorous poem. When she was ready to record (not when I said she was ready), we recorded, then played the piece back. Before I was aware of what was happening, she was following along with the book, correcting her errors, then asking to re-record. She read passages backward, and how she laughed at the meaningless sentences coming back at her. She developed a love for poetry and entered the school's poetry reading contest, won first, then went on to win the district contest. She has gone on to prose at her grade level. Angie's spark plugs had become clogged by too many people pushing her too hard. Once the dirt of pressure—the I can't—was cleaned out, she picked up speed and interest.

I use the recorder in classroom reading sessions. The children record in unison, then we play back. Each child tries hard, *wanting* to be perfect. One day as the class left the reading center, one child patted the recorder lovingly. "Teacher, take good care of our friend. Don't drop him or lose him." This child had entered my classroom on the slow-slow list.

We are reminded Thomas Edison was considered retarded. Fuller, the mathematician, was considered a misfit. And who can forget Helen Keller with her multitude of handicaps? A sculptor is said to have remarked, "I don't carve a statue. I release the figure buried within the marble." And the Master Teacher, Jesus, tried to make people realize their own potentials.

Not all children classified as mentally retarded are as fortunate as Joyce, the actress was—to have been discovered by someone who saw her worth and released the beautiful figure within. But with patience, innovation, we can decrease the unfortunate numbers. There can be no re-run of the film of childhood.

Lord,

We thank You for the opportunity of serving You today. In our classrooms, help us to put right above self-interest.

May we put matters of spirit before material. Grant that we may bring happiness where there is none, encouragement where there is discouragement.

May we always follow the example of Your Son Jesus in all our associations with the children of our classrooms.

For being with us, we give thanks. Amen.

13—Guard Your Thoughts

Psalm 85:10: *"Mercy and truth are met together; righteousness and peace have kissed each other."*
Proverbs 15:13: *"A merry heart maketh a cheerful countenance: but by sorrow of the heart the spirit is broken."*
John 4:14: *"Whosoever drinketh of the water that I shall give him shall never thirst; but the water that I shall give him shall be in him a well of water springing up into everlasting life."*

One day while I was walking along the aisle of a large department store, an elderly lady turned into the same aisle and headed toward me. She wore a large hat topped with huge bright red roses. She wore a chiffon scarf printed with pink roses. On the shoulder of her blue suit jacket she wore, you're right, two more roses.

Oh, I thought involuntarily, I wish she had better taste. She could be such an attractive person.

Just as the woman came even with me, and we were face to face, then passing, she stuck out her foot, tripping me. I fell flat on my face. The floorman and salespeople rushed to my assistance. "Are you hurt?" they asked.

I exclaimed, "That woman deliberately tripped me. I saw her!"

Physically, I was not injured. But I was emotionally and psychologically hurt. I knew I had allowed my feelings and thoughts for the woman to show in my face. Is that why she had tripped me?

During the following weeks I hardly dared look at anyone

directly. And I certainly refrained from having adverse opinions on any subjects. I didn't want to fall on my face again as a result of negative thoughts.

When I was in elementary school, our class was presided over by Miss Jason, who often wore a blouse of violent colors and patterns. We soon learned that that blouse indicated she was having one of her bad days. "Watch out!" we warned each other. "Miss Jason is wearing *that* blouse again!" The slightest misstep brought swift and severe punishment down on our heads.

I inadvertently, and certainly unconsciously, fell into a dark mood trap. I had troublesome problems in my personal life. I frequently wore a two-toned gray knit outfit to school. I liked it (then), felt comfortable in it. But Mike, one of my students, ruined it for me. "Teacher, whenever you wear that dress I always know you're going to be in a bad mood. I guess you bring your bad feelings to school with it." Before I could make a caustic remark about rudeness, I did some quick thinking. I remembered the woman in the store.

No doubt we teachers belong to the same family as that long ago Miss Jason. Our personal affairs do get out of line. Since we are human, we awaken with stuffy noses. We have extra home problems—pipes break, we have unexpected dental bills. Someone steps on our sensitive toes. Our safety is threatened in one way or another. Unconsciously we carry these problems with us into the schoolroom.

What can we do to prevent ourselves from being the villain in the classroom?

As for myself, I now take a little extra time for my regular morning devotions. I close my eyes, relax my mind and body. I picture my mind being emptied of the troublesome thoughts, worries and problems I had with my breakfast. As soon as I feel relaxed, I re-read my morning devotional article. When the one for that particular date does not satisfy my need, I search for one which does.

I read a special verse. "Put on the whole armour of God . . ." (Ephesians 6:11). Slowly my emptied mind refills with more positive and helpful thoughts. My defenses against a hard day in the classroom are built.

But I dare not stop at that.

Things happen in the classroom. A child may have

wakened with a stuffy nose too. He will not, or cannot, do his work. He trips a little girl going down the aisle past him. Now my warming-up exercises of the morning are put to the test. If I don't like my reaction to his misdeed, I redirect my thinking. I say, "I know, Andy, your foot just happened to be in the aisle and Susan didn't see it. But please say you're sorry." Andy, his feelings saved, readily apologizes.

A child spills his milk at lunchtime. Teacher's impulse is to be impatient. But the ideal is: When something goes wrong, say something right. The right is, "We can clean up the milk and the spot on the floor will be cleaner afterward."

Martie breaks a clay relief map. The teacher at first thinks only of the work involved and now gone for nothing. Again, the ideal: "We can start over and build a better map." With these kind and understanding responses, we avoid tripping, and being tripped.

Friends remark of a certain teacher, "She is the kind who has her whole life smiling in front of her! How easy it is to see Christ in her!" The ideal!

I wish I could be like her. I'm always trying!

Gracious and ever-listening Lord,

Help us to gift-wrap our troubles and worries in the happy colors of gentleness and understanding. Though inwardly we may not always be as happy as we would prefer, we ask that we never ruin another's day with our own dark moods.

We know that a cheerful smile will bring a smile back to us.

We are rewarded by the use of the strength, the knowledge You have given us through the towering presence of Your Son.

Thank You for courage, for strength. Thank You for the faces of happy children. Amen.

14—I Think Of Mary*

Luke 2:7: *"And she brought forth her firstborn son, and wrapped him in swaddling clothes, and laid him in a manger; because there was no room for them in the inn."*
Job 39:12: *"Wilt thou believe him, that he will bring home thy seed, and gather it into thy barn?"*
Psalm 78:52: *"But made his own people to go forth like sheep, and guided them in the wilderness like a flock."*

In our yearly celebrations of Christmas, our attentions are centered upon the birth of Jesus, whose life has influenced mankind more than that of any other person. But what of Mary, His mother?

Now, I think especially of her.

During the holiday season, I was driving to a distant state to begin a teaching position in January. I was alone, frightened. Sorrowing too, for I had recently been left alone. "Don't go," my friends said. "At your age you shouldn't be going to a strange place."

But I could not resist the offer. The position, that of teaching exceptional children, was something I wanted to do. I felt the need to serve.

The excitement, the urge to resettle myself, carried me through the first two days of the long journey which led me across a stretch of desert land. Chains of red-rock pinnacled mountains skirting the highway, the tang of sage after a brief

* From *Evangel*, December 1970, used by permission of Light and Life Press.

shower, a giant jack rabbit scurrying across the sand were all exhilarating. I drove through little desert towns whose box-front stores reminded me of pictures of pioneer days. Christmas tinsels and bells glittered in the sunlight.

Then late one afternoon I ran into a desert storm. As I sped on, with rain slashing across the windshield, I became frightened. A sense of lostness, of complete alienation from the world gripped me. Desert flash flooding was another worry. Had I, after all, made a mistake in leaving the security of my hometown?

I passed through still another desert town, no more than a store and gas station. Beside a small house, the bright colors of a large creche, washed by driving rain, caught my attention. But it was the figure of Mary, the mother of Jesus, whose face I saw in particular.

I carried the reflected image of her in my mind's eyes as I sped on into the swift darkness of a stormy desert night— Mary's face radiating a supreme faith, an all-embodying serenity. How had she really felt? I began to wonder. Had she been afraid as she journeyed on the donkey toward Bethlehem that night so many centuries ago? What had been her thoughts? She knew the birth of her child was near. Where would she stay? Who would be in that place to care for her? Could even the faithful Joseph, plodding at her side, still her fears, stop the drumming of her heart? Is there anything written of her that does not reveal quiet courage, complete acquiescence to the will of God? I decided there was nothing. Taking courage, I sped on.

I began to see signs announcing the nearness of my destination. Heavy rain continued to pour down, and I lost all sense of direction as I searched for the motel where I had made reservations to stay until I could find a place to live permanently. At last the motel's blinking sign appeared ahead of me. But inside the office, I found there had been a mix-up. No room had been reserved for me.

The overworked clerk began phoning around to other places for me. But each time he shook his head. "They're all full. It's Christmastime, you know."

Again I was compelled to think of Mary. Had she waited patiently when she found she had no immediate shelter? Had fear churned within her, fears that muzzled her mind so that she could not think straight? And did she feel the growing intensity of pain, warning her of the impending birth of the Child? I closed my eyes and prayed, even as she must have prayed, "Dear God, let there be a place."

I opened my eyes, unclenched my hands. The room spun around me. "Isn't there any place?" I asked the clerk. I did not think of calling the principal of my new school.

The harassed clerk pulled at his ear. "There might be a place at Mrs. Brown's. She takes in roomers." He phoned.

My prayer was answered and soon I was shown into a small, clean though sparsely furnished room. Now, again, my thoughts returned to Mary. Shelter at last, warm shelter from the storm. A special supper tray prepared by the kind landlady was delivered to me. Had Mary had supper that night?

I unpacked my bag, and there in one corner of it lay a gift-wrapped package. The friend who had helped me with last-minute packing had tucked it in there, I knew. I unwrapped it. It was a pine-scented candle in a colored glass container. I placed it on the chest and lighted it. Soon tangy fragrance filled the room. What kind of light had Mary had that night?

Next morning I called the principal of my school. "Oh, we're so happy you're here!" she exclaimed. "We worried about you driving in that storm. Now we want you to spend Christmas Eve with us. And one of our board members, Mr. Johnson, wants you to be with him and his family Christmas Day. . . ."

"I couldn't possibly impose. . . ." Had Mary had a false pride that forced her to refuse hospitality?

"You're part of our church family. You're at home," my principal said graciously.

My mind returned to Mary again and again that evening as I joined and became part of my principal's family circle. I thought of her again on Christmas Day at the friendly Johnson's home. They presented me with a package of fruits—dates, figs, oranges, grown in the vicinity. Then they set another package before me. "These are gifts from the children of your new class, made especially for you before their teacher left," Mrs. Johnson, a gentle happy-faced woman told me.

"But I can't. . . ." My objections at being the recipient of so much thoughtfulness from strangers rose without a thought. Then came to mind, "and when they had opened their treasures, they presented unto him gifts; gold, and frankincense, and myrrh . . ." (Matthew 2:11). Had Mary, ashamed of her needs, attempted to refuse the precious gifts of goodwill from generous loving hearts to her Son? I was certain she had not.

Joy, a feeling of security, of knowing I had found a new home among people who would surely be my friends suddenly became part of my heart and mind. I was home again.

That is why, now, I think of Mary.

Kind Heavenly Father,

Today, I feel a growing thankfulness that so many people are necessary to me; that a deeper knowledge of Christ is now in my mind. Through Christ I know that as this appreciation and knowledge grow, I am more able to follow the Christian path of giving more love and understanding and service to others.

In spirit I kneel in adoration and present the gift of my talents, whatever they may be, to others in need, even as I have been supplied with substance to fulfill my own needs.

Forgive the sometimes faltering of my faith. Lift me into the world of Your blessings. Amen.

15—"But Didn't The Camels Get Thirsty?"*

Psalm 94:10: *"He that chastiseth the heathen, shall not he be correct? he that teacheth man knowledge, shall not he know?"*

Psalm 119:66: *"Teach me good judgment and knowledge: for I have believed thy commandments."*

Colossians 1:9: *"For this cause we also, since the day we heard it, do not cease to pray for you, and to desire that ye might be filled with the knowledge of his will in all wisdom and spiritual understanding."*

Memories of my own childhood hearing of Bible stories are vivid. Morning devotions consisted of endless reading of the Bible by a slow-speaking, near-sighted grandmother who even found inspiration in the "begats!"

How often my restless eyes turned to the window where the wind-driven snow pounded. How long would it be before I could get into heavy coat and mittens and go out to put my new sled into action?

These memories made me determined to inspire the children of my classroom to think of the Bible as fascinating, not dull. I experimented endlessly, using in turn, flannelboard stories, or simply telling the stories, making up drama and dialogue as I went along. This was good, but not good

---

* Reprinted by permission from *Sunday School Leader,* © 1965, David C. Cook Publishing Co., Elgin, Ill.

enough. I saw reflections of my own childhood lack of interest on the faces of the children before me.

There must be another method to make God's Word come alive. I asked the Lord to guide me.

One morning I was telling the story of Abraham's sending his steward to the city of Haran, home of his brother, Nahor. The servant was to find a wife for Isaac. I stood near the chalkboard, and with some unrecognized instinct for the dramatic I marked off the path the servant and his convoy might have taken to Canaan.

Since the students knew how hot and dry our California deserts can be, I sketched in bare desert mountains, clouds of sand rising beneath the camels' feet, the sun beating down. I roughed in stick camels and robed people.

For the first time I put myself in the place of those ancient people. I knew something of the difficult trip—the fear of bandits, the heat, the grit of sand between my teeth, the utter weariness of man and beast.

My feelings must have communicated themselves to the children, for not a chair creaked. Suddenly, during my pause for breath, Debra asked, "But didn't the camels get thirsty?"

The perfect place for a science lesson! I explained that God had provided in the walls of camels' stomachs, chambers where they can store a supply of water for use when none is available.

Now, while I had interest, we moved into Bible customs. I drew a picture of a typical well of those times. They had never seen such a well. To them, water came from a tap. They knew about lakes, rivers, but not wells.

Next we talked about Rebecca's filling the crock (with explanation of that utensil) and giving the camels water. The servant noticed this act of kindness. This led him to choose her for Isaac's wife.

I learned a lesson that day. A child's inattention may stem from the fact that he knows nothing of the meaning of words the teacher often uses. My drawing more than compensated for that.

"But I can't draw!" a teacher may protest.

Children love crude drawings, perhaps because they are on a level with their own creativity. Stickmen fascinate them. Their imaginations make up for what the stickmen lack.

When we studied Moses' leading the Israelites out of Egypt, with Pharaoh's armies in pursuit, my two opposing clusters of vertical lines to depict the enemy soldiers brought gasps and outcries. The picture of the Red Sea divided became, on the chalkboard, just so many curved lines forming walls through which the people might pass. But it was sufficient.

In preparing Bible lessons, I made it a rule never to plan the picture I would draw. There's always a right moment, a right idea. I began to draw when my own emotions were touched through one or more of the five senses. After all, to taste, to touch, to see, to hear, to smell (even in imagination) makes up the tendrils by which we experience life. In drawing at this right moment, my emotions were communicated to the children.

Some stories lend themselves to illustration more easily than others. Joseph's experience with his brothers was a natural. So was David and Goliath. One boy's enthusiasm went so far as to impel him to bring a slingshot to school!

When we discussed how Biblical people made bricks, two class members got together on Saturday and with coarse weeds and mud fashioned some bricks and brought them to school later. That was something concrete to remember.

Next, I asked the children to draw their own ideas of what might have happened. I asked about Joseph's coat. Was it striped, polka dot? Did it have a striped border? Was it long or short? As many variations as there were students were produced.

Later, we formed teams and the teams competed in producing a mural—the garden of Eden, Jesus teaching little children.

When time arrived to present the Christmas story, the experience was as deeply moving for me as for the children. Sketching as I talked, the experience of the Wise Men truly came alive to me. I had been on the desert on cold nights. I had smelled its fragrance, shivered at the sound of a distant animal's cry.

As I told the story, it seemed to me I could actually see the eyes of the Wise Men turn toward the brightest star of all in the black sky. I felt the emotions of those men as later they knelt before the Babe of Bethlehem and as they talked about the star that led them there to worship. And wasn't I even hearing the child's early cries, as if already He were aware of what His life would come to? Realism was being communicated to me and through me.

I finished the story. There was silence in the room momentarily. What finally broke the silence? A spontaneous singing of one child, joined by thirty others. "Silent Night! Holy Night!" they sang softly.

The magic of that eternally precious time had come down through the ages to us with the help of chalk sketching people and camels at the right time.

The Lord had His own way of leading me in the selection of a right way to inspire the children of this class.

Dear Lord,

Today we thank You for the opportunities to use our hands and our minds for the enlightenment of little children. We know they are dear to You.

We are thankful You have chosen us to spread Your word. May we always use our mind and hearts to Your glory. Amen.

16—Creative Mouse Traps*

II Chronicles 30:22: "And Hezekiah spake comfortably unto all the Levites that taught the good knowledge of the Lord: and they did eat throughout the feast of seven days, offering peaceofferings, and making confession to the Lord God of their fathers."

Proverbs 20:11: "Even a child is known by his doings, whether his work be pure, and whether it be right."

Isaiah 11:9: "They shall not hurt nor destroy in all my holy mountain: for the earth shall be full of the knowledge of the Lord, as the waters cover the sea."

Arriving early, Mrs. Ann Ryder hid pieces of cheese in her second grade classroom. Judy and Charles arrived with traps and rubber mice. "What's this about?" Charles asked. The teacher smiled mysteriously.

Other students arrived, some bringing rubber mice and traps. They were curious, excited.

The Bible lesson today was based on Matthew 4, Jesus' fasting and temptation. The teacher then asked the children to repeat the last section. Then she baited the traps with the cheese.

Mrs. Ryder said, "Each of you push your mouse around a trap. Careful! Imagine the mouse hasn't eaten for days. Bring him closer, to the trap."

* Reprinted by permission from *Sunday School Leader*, © 1965, David C. Cook Publishing Co., Elgin, Ill.

Walt said, "He's scared. He got caught once, but got loose, and . . ."

"Will he give in to temptation?" Deftly the teacher used the key word "temptation" from the day's lesson.

"Hey!" Rick said. "If the mouse gives in he'll get into trouble." He let his mouse give in. Others didn't.

"This is activity teaching," Mrs. Ryder explained. "The child performs and learns."

"At first," she went on, "I demonstrated. But when we had the Moses and the burning bush lesson, I was doing the illustrating on the chalkboard and Ruth begged, 'Let me do it.' I watched her. Then another child asked to help. 'I want to do the bush that kept on burning.' From then on I let them create."

Ask Forrest his favorite story. After some thought, he says, "Moses." He points to the map showing the Exodus journey. "I wish I coulda been Moses. He heard God's word from the burning bush. Mrs. Ryder brought a staff with a hook on it. When she said shut our eyes, we did. She threw down the staff like God told Moses to. When we looked, there was a rubber snake. We shut our eyes again and opened them. There was the staff. That sure taught Moses he wanted God as a partner when he rescued the Israelites from those Egyptians!"

To illustrate how Christians thrive spiritually if they do not hoard their affections and talents, the children drew pictures of the Sea of Galilee and the Red Sea. The teacher asked, "Where does the Dead Sea water go after it comes from the Sea of Galilee?"

A girl replied, "Nowhere. It dries up."

"What happens if we hide our treasures?"

"Nothing. I guess that's why I'm happy when I share."

Christmas activity was remembered delight. Each child brought a small birthday candle. At the appropriate time Teacher set a little box, wrapped in white, before each child. After the story of Christ's birth, the children opened the boxes. Inside was a card. On it was printed John 3:16: "For God so loved the world. . . ."

A child exclaimed, "Why, God gave us Jesus. He was born and we were born too. That's why we brought the candles."

Mrs. Ryder brought out white cupcakes, the children

decorated them with candles, and the class sang a Christmas song honoring the Christ-child.

For the lesson taught by Psalm 23, the teacher, with her faithful staff, took the children outside. She asked them to walk on all fours around her. When someone got out of line, she gently drew him back with the crook of the staff. When a mischievous girl went flat, she lifted her. "I am the good shepherd. I take care of you as God does all of us." Now "The Lord is my shepherd" means more to them.

A parent often asks Mrs. Ryder, "Don't you ever run out of ideas?"

"Of course!" She smiles. "But I close my eyes, open my mind to all the beautiful teachings of the Bible and God always gives me ideas. Often too, I just imagine I am a child, eager to know what all the lessons in the Bible really mean."

Mrs. Ryder asked questions of herself. Has she allowed the lessons to be buried in seas of activity? "The children will probably remember the stories or lessons," she says, "but if they have not understood them, then applied them in their daily lives, I will have failed them and God."

Ever-present God,

We thank You that Your love for us causes us to stretch our minds so we can bring Your Word to little children.

As we reach out in our teaching to those in our care, may we always be aware You are reaching out to us, helping us, inspiring us through our daily communion with You.

As we go our way this day be with us. Amen.

17—The B and F Club Is In Session*

Psalm 132:12: *"If thy children will keep my covenant and my testimony that I shall teach them, their children shall also sit up on thy throne for evermore."*
Matthew 14:16: *"But Jesus said unto them, They need not depart; give ye them to eat."*
Mark 6:34: *"And Jesus, when he came out, saw much people, and was moved with compassion toward them, because they were as sheep not having a shepherd: and he began to teach them many things."*

David, an eight-year-old third grader in the Christian elementary school, rose, walked purposefully to the front of the room as soon as Bible lesson ended. "The meeting of the B and F Club will now come to order," he said to the attentive children. The teacher took a seat at the back of the room.

The club, adhering to *Robert's Rules of Order,* began its weekly session.

Eight-year-olds conducting a meeting! What was this B and F Club? It sounded like a cough drop society.

The teacher had been in this room more than two years. Dutifully, devotedly, each day the Bible lessons had been presented. Visual aids were used to spice up the lessons. But the teacher felt increasingly disappointed with results from a learning standpoint.

"I realized though," the teacher confessed, "I was teaching

* Reprinted from *Interaction,* by permission of Concordia Publishing House.

the children *about* the Bible and Christianity, but not *how* to be Christians."

One day during morning devotions, the teacher read Matthew 14, the account of Jesus feeding the multitudes, and paused to think over the story, to meditate on its deep meaning.

This thought came: the feeding of the multitudes doesn't necessarily relate to the nourishment of bodies. It can relate to feeding people spiritually and emotionally too. Isn't that what Jesus meant when He said, "Love one another?" Why couldn't this insight be shared with the children, and let it inspire them.

Knowing children love secrets and can keep them, the teacher presented the following plan to the class the next week.

"Boys and girls, how would you like to have a club of your own? A secret club." The class had been restless, anxious for a quick getaway. Now members perked up.

"What kind of club?" asked Steven warily.

"You remember the story of Jesus feeding the multitudes? Well, to be His followers we don't necessarily have to feed people food. We can show them love by helping them," replied the teacher.

"Helping who?" asked Tanya.

Now the plan unfolded. The club would be called the B and F Club, the letters standing for bread and fish. The members would perform kind deeds instead of giving food.

"I help my mother with the baby when she *makes* me," said Cindy.

"I have to carry out the rubbish," grumbled Tom.

"Think how exciting it would be if we really *wanted* to do these things in a loving way," the teacher added, then outlined the plan. And it was immediately adopted into action.

Each Monday after Bible lesson, the secret club met. The children took turns presiding. They also took turns reading Matthew 14:13,21, as a reminder of Jesus' work and His kindnesses to people. They prayed for Jesus to live in them, and to use them to serve people.

The club motto became, "Love one another," with the password, "Emmanuel," which means "God is with us."

At the meetings each member reported what he had done for others during the week. There were no rewards for doing things and no club pins since the club was secret.

Later the teacher commented, "Though I had some doubt about the children's capacity to remember, such fears soon left me. Some parents went through a period of shock at the change in the children's attitudes.

It took some time for the children to learn proper meeting procedures, but then all went well.

David reported at the first meeting: "It took me a while to get with it, but now I take the rubbish out pretty often. My dad says he doesn't know what hit me. I even get ahead of him Saturdays when he's tired and pull weeds."

A girl reported, "I thought my mother would faint when I said I'd do the dishes. Next I'm going to clean my room without being asked."

Steve said, "You know that crabby old man next door to us? I never liked him. Finally I decided to bring his paper to him one morning. You know, he's real friendly after all. He even gave me a dime for doing it. It's hard for him to walk. I didn't take the dime either."

Jerry added, "I almost spilled the club secret when I stopped a fight between some kids on my way home Sunday. They wanted to know why I was butting in. But I caught myself and just said Jesus taught we ought to love one another. They laughed like crazy. I noticed though they forgot to go on fighting."

Another girl revealed she had helped a classmate when she was having trouble with arithmetic and that another time she stayed in the office with a sick friend waiting for her mother to come.

Slowly it went at first, but then more regularly good deeds were done with enthusiasm, in secret, without expectation of reward, except for the warming of their thoughts and hearts. And surprisingly, the eight-year-olds really learned the rules of order and how to use them in His name.

The short snappy meetings closed with heads bowed, the children repeating a prayer the teacher had written especially for them:

God, come into my mind and into my thoughts.
Come into my eyes so I may see good to do.
Watch my mouth so I may speak kindly.
God, be in my heart today, tomorrow, always.

Then everyone whispered, "Emmanuel—God be with us."

Dear Lord,

Today I would think not only of myself, and pray not only for myself, as I seek this moment of quiet. I think now of the children in my charge.

I pray especially for those who do not know Your ways, who have never been taught Your ways.

Make me, Heavenly Father, a human channel through Your love so that I may reach others and bring them into the fold of Christian life. I do give thanks for all blessings, for all opportunities to bring happiness to others. Amen.

18—Where Two Are Gathered Together

James 5:13-15: *"Is any among you afflicted? let him pray. Is any merry? let him sing psalms. Is any sick among you? let him call for the elders of the church; and let them pray over him, anointing him with oil in the name of the Lord. And the prayer of faith shall save the sick, and the Lord shall raise him up; and if he have committed sins, they shall be forgiven him."*
John 14:13: *"And whatsoever ye shall ask in my name, that will I do, that the Father may be glorified in the Son."*

The time—8:15 Monday morning. The place—the kitchen of the parish hall connected with the Christian day school. The six teachers and the principal were gathered, sipping coffee, lacing their fingers around the mugs as though they were trying to find warmth for their troubled minds and hearts. The activity—morning prayers. It had not always been this way.

At first there was general conversation of the weather, of home problems, of problem children at school.

Now, Mrs. Carniff of second grade said, "I don't know what to do about Linda. She's supposed to take her medication at noon. I stand by and watch her, but she nearly always tricks me, pretending to swallow it, but later spits it out. She's driving me up the wall."

"Perhaps Linda needs praying over today," suggested Mr. Topping, the principal.

"Her teacher needs praying over as much as Linda," Mrs. Carniff said shortly.

Morning coffee-prayers. They became the much needed staff-of-life for the faculty of our school. Early in the term the rumor was that a cross-town freeway might take away most of our limited playground space. "I believe daily prayers would let God know we have a real problem," suggested Mr. Topping at one of our faculty devotional meetings held in the library twice a week. General school problems were also worked out at these meetings.

"We teachers need God's help as much as our school," said Miss Crandall of fourth grade. "Why don't we pray at coffee time?" She quoted Philippians 4:13, "I can do all things through Christ which strengtheneth me."

So the prayers—informal as they were, yet no less sincere—began.

We stood silent as if by common consent, waiting for the sense of peace which comes from God to settle over us. Often many minutes passed before the feeling came. Then slowly a feeling of peace, of warmth, of rightness came over us. Someone began to pray as he or she felt led.

We were still concerned over the proposed freeway project. There had been no decision. What would our school do without the playground? One morning Mr. Topping said, "I think we're a lot like the man during the sugar rationing period of WWII, who asked the waitress for more sugar in his morning coffee. 'Just stir up the sugar that's already in the bottom of your cup, sir,' she told him crisply."

We needed more of that sugar-faith.

At last the freeway problem was settled. Only a small corner of our property would go. But, and here's where God's design came in: There would be a high embankment, covered with shrubs and fenced off. Some of our children who were always running to that corner and skipping away would no longer be able to do that. God knew best.

There were other prayer requests. A little boy fell while swinging, cutting his head badly, and was rushed to the hospital. We prayed for him.

One of our teachers had a teenage son whom she feared

was on drugs. "I've prayed, but nothing happens. I question him, but we both get angry," she wept.

We prayed for the son and for the mother to exercise gentle Christian understanding. Later, the teacher commented, "Just knowing you were praying, understanding, helped me to relax and pray. To be more gentle with my son. Things are better now."

The bus driver stormed in one morning just as we began prayers. "I'm quitting! Those Darnell kids are driving me out of my skull!"

"We're having prayers, Jim," Mr. Topping said. "Join us."

He stayed. Afterward, he said, "The steam's all taken out of me. With God's help, I'll handle them."

Another day the maintenance man interrupted. "Someone soaped my clean windows last night. If I could just get hold of . . ." He stopped short at the sight of the sound of prayers. He listened, then went away to rewash windows. He was whistling.

Sometimes we made no requests in prayer time and simply repeated Psalm 23 in unison. Sometimes we were silent, making ourselves receptive only to the still small voice of God, being grateful to the beauty of nearby mountains and merely contemplating the words from Psalm 121, "I will lift up my eyes unto the hills, from whence cometh my help." Or, "Thank you Lord, for all blessings." We went about our duties refreshed, prepared to meet the day's problems.

One boy told his mother about the teachers praying together over coffee. A new dimension was added. The boy lived in a racially integrated neighborhood. The mother called Mr. Topping.

"Johnny told me about you teachers praying over coffee, relying on God. I did some thinking, Mr. Topping. Some of us women here get together mornings after our men leave. All we've ever done is gripe about our neighbors and what the place is coming to. We decided to pray, then listen to God's will for us. We're praying together, and I mean *all* of us. It's made a big difference. We're understanding more about practicing loving one another. We've all got problems. Just sharing them helps. Now we get along fine."

So the kitchen prayers also branched out into neighborhood prayers.

Heavenly Father,

We know You keep the stars in their courses; we know You are their designer. We know that as time goes on You reveal Your plans, and as we ask, so shall we receive.

May our ways always be made clear by You. May our minds always be set upon Your graciousness, Your givingness. If we wait patiently and in perfect faith, we know You will make known to us Your answer to our needs.

For Your promises to us, Your children, we are always grateful. Amen.

19—One More Step*

Psalm 25:4: *"Shew me thy ways, O Lord; teach me thy paths."*
Psalm 145:14: *"The Lord upholdeth all that fall, and raiseth up all those that be bowed down."*
I Corinthians 3:8, 9: *"Now he that planteth and he that watereth are one: and every man shall receive his own award according to his labour. For we are labourers together with God: ye are God's husbandry, ye are God's building."*

As I approached the Woodland Street address, even my car seemed to hold back. And it wasn't the cold weather. What was I letting myself in for? I was about to begin a new untried field of teaching. "God be with me," I prayed.

The previous evening my phone had rung. "Are you the teacher at the Christian school?" a high-pitched voice asked. "A member of your church said if anyone can help my Judy, you can. She's rated EMR (educable mentally retarded). I know she can learn, if I can just find the right teacher." She began sobbing. "I used to believe in God, that He would help me, but now—" She lost control, recovered. "Judy's twelve years old!"

Teach a mentally retarded child? Sometimes in discouraging times I wondered if I could teach normal children.

In spite of the negative feelings, I felt a quickening pulse. The retarded child's problems, and those of the parents too,

* From *Purpose*, March 1967, published by Mennonite Publishing House.

had interested me. For a time I'd substituted in a school for the retarded. My library contained many books on mental retardation and how to deal with it. I'd even applied some of the recommended techniques of teaching in my own classroom of normal children. Yet, as I listened to this distraught mother, I hesitated. Suppose I harmed rather than helped this child?

"Please!" she begged. "You do so much for the children in your classroom." Her desperation (and no doubt the flattery) made me say I'd try.

Now here I was at the home. Mrs. Childers was small, dark, in her late thirties and extremely tense.

"Judy!" she called shrilly. "Your teacher is here!"

We found short, plump Judy crouching behind a chair. Her large dark eyes seemed filled with countless fears. She rubbed her hands together continuously.

I followed the two into the den where the mother had provided a table, pencils and paper. But my plans disintegrated into chaos.

Mrs. Childers showed me a coloring book filled with scrawls a two-year-old might have done. "*That's* four months' work!"

Pity for this mother who realized her child's problems as she developed, and those of herself as age came on her made me say, "We'll just take it one step at a time."

Judy, making little cooing sounds, fingered my sweater.

I persuaded her to sit beside me. Silently, I committed myself to God's direction. His power is available to us all. I knew I could tap that power. I relaxed.

"Will you count for me, Judy?"

"She can't count," the mother said.

"Let's count, Judy," I repeated.

The child giggled. The mother said, "She always does that."

"Perhaps Judy would be less distracted if I try with her alone." The mother, with a sigh, left. We began again.

Twisting her plump hands, she began, "One, two, three, four, five . . . seven, eight, nine, ten." She began again, skipping "six" as before.

I reached into my case and brought out an egg carton, a bag of marbles and a set of large green letters of the alphabet. I dumped the marbles into a plastic bowl. "Judy, you put one

marble into each pocket of the carton and count as you do."
Though I felt breathless, I kept my voice low-pitched.

She began again. "One." She dropped one marble. She
went through five, but jumped to seven again. She began to
giggle. It was time for a change.

I showed her the green letters, asked her to name them.
Some she could not, or would not, name.

I was aware of the mother hovering out of sight, so I was
relieved when the hour was over. There was just no hope, I
decided. The mother looked at me anxiously. "Please don't
give up," she begged. "I'm on tranquilizers and coffee. My
husband and I are quarreling. Our son hates his sister. But I
know he's ashamed of her."

How could I refuse? I remembered a line from Sir Francis
Bacon. "There is more lost in not trying than there is in not
succeeding."

At home, I prepared an award book. I mounted a sheet of
white paper on red construction paper, marked it off in
squares. When Judy did well, I'd permit her to stamp a square
with a cartoon character from a collection I'd gotten from a
cereal company for a box top and coins.

It took some doing to explain to Judy about the stamps, but
she soon got the idea.

I restudied the methods Jesus, the Master Teacher used. He
began with the point where people were at the time. When
they had absorbed one lesson, he went on to a new idea, step
by step. I thought: I'll take Judy step by step too. When she
has learned one thing, I'll lead her to the next. I kept this in
mind at each lesson, being more and more thankful for the
lessons I had learned from God's Word.

At last! Judy broke through and counted to ten without
error. I was so elated I let her stamp an entire row of cartoon
characters in the award book.

The alphabet was more difficult. We stood rooted on this
plateau when I read an account of Doctor Carl K. Becker, the
Congo missionary. When the rebel forces during those tragic
days of the early sixties were nearing Oicha, he was urged to
flee. But one of his favorite Bible verses made him remain.
"Fear ye not," he read from Exodus 14:13, "stand still, and see
the salvation of the Lord . . ." Well, if Doctor Becker could

hold fast in time of grave danger, I could certainly hold fast with Judy.

Finally I realized the letters themselves meant nothing to her and borrowed a first grade phonics book. To my amazement, she had concepts of pictures. I put the green letters together to spell the name of an animal. Soon she began to recognize letters and words. The mother reported, Judy spelled words while she ate.

Now she could count to 200 without help. But we still used the marbles for basic addition and substraction.

Came then, the memorable day, almost a year later when she took up the pre-primer. That took patience and many prayers on my part too. She took her book everywhere and read to anyone who would listen!

To add to the triumph, the entire family, including the brother, found excitement and joy in helping her. They also found the power of God through her accomplishments.

How far could I take her? I didn't know. But I remembered Doctor Becker. I remembered Jesus' patience in teaching. I looked at Judy who had stepped from the pages of the books I had read on helping the retarded. She was learning. We, together, with God's help, took still another step.

Dear Lord,

I feel anxious and inadequate today. I ask of You: Let me follow in the footsteps of the Master, wherever they may lead me.

Let my thinking be keen, my speech open and tender; my actions courageous.

Keep my hands and voice gentle with patience.

For all these blessings You have given me in Your service, I give thanks. Amen.

20—What's In The Bible?

Psalm 68:11: *"The Lord gave the word: great was the company of those that published it."*
Isaiah 9:8: *"The Lord sent the word into Jacob, and it hath lighted upon Israel."*
Matthew 4:4: *"But he answered and said, It is written, Man shall not live by bread alone, but by every word that proceedeth out of the mouth of God."*

Mr. Lee Fong, a fourth grade teacher, was disturbed. At teachers' meeting, he related, "I asked the class what is in the Bible. What replies I got! One little girl said, 'My baby picture, a letter from my grandmother and my mother and father's wedding picture.' " His Oriental face wore a look of shock.

Mr. Fong had come from Singapore to live in the United States so his daughter could have a Christian education. He had been principal of a large Christian school at home.

His consternation sent the teachers scurrying to their classrooms to investigate their own students' beliefs.

The second grade teacher reported, "Jeaninne said they never read the Bible. John said, 'We have Bible reading every night, but nobody talks about it. I sometimes go to sleep. I don't understand the words.' "

The fifth grade teacher reported better results. "My children said the Bible is God's Word. It tells us to love our enemies. But another said, 'How can you love somebody who socks you? I guess there weren't kids that socked you back then . . .' They don't get the point."

Putting family letters, keepsakes and admonition aside, the teachers began looking for real answers to Mr. Fong's question, "What's in the Bible?"

No doubt there are many adults as well as children who have read the Bible as far as the end of Genesis, perhaps a scattering of Psalms, probed the words of Jesus, but they have no real understanding of the entire Bible. They have no system of applying its teachings to their daily lives.

But there is literally everything in the Bible. Anyone who seeks identification with God and His teachings—love, conviction, forgiveness, guidance—can find it. It just takes work.

Mr. Fong and the teachers realized this as they further discussed this serious gap in the children's education. True, there were daily Bible lessons. True, the lessons were vividly portrayed with maps, Bible memory verses and rules of conduct set up according to the Word. But how could they make the children *understand*?

The teachers developed a series of guidelines. The points were to be presented not as a whole, but bit by bit as the occasion arose.

1. Psalm 119:33 begins, "Teach me, O Lord." We must always approach the Bible prayerfully as the inspired Word of God. This opens our minds so we really listen to its teachings. From youth to advanced age it is our treasured possession. As an example of this devotion and faithfulness, we should remember Sir Walter Scott, the author of many great works, remarked on his death bed, "The only real book is the Bible."

2. The Bible was set down by "holy men of God." They were moved by the Spirit. They were in constant communication with that Spirit through prayers, through faith.

3. If the meaning is clear, there is no reason for searching out some secret, symbolic one. It is a matter of semantics. But it is well to check the translation of words. For instance, the word "suffer" when taken from the King James version, sometimes means to permit. "Conversation" meant manner of life. "Charity" meant to show affection or concern.

4. God gave His Word as recorded in the Bible to and through human beings. They were of different stations of life, and spoke in their own idioms. The Apostle John wrote in Greek and he wrote in plain language. Luke was a physician. Paul, whose background was Judaism, majored on the grace of God. James was very practical.

5. We can take comfort that the early church had problems just as present-day churches do. Some were divided over their ministers, others over immorality. There were divisions over marriages, over idolatry, the conduct of women in society. Doesn't that all sound familiar?

6. Read and study the texts. Try to write out what truths you found in them and then practice these truths in your own life.

7. Try to apply Bible truths to the children's lives as guidelines for living the Christian life. Use real-life examples. Make the lessons so real the children will leave the classroom remembering so well they will not "sock the enemy right back." They will, instead, give understanding, love. Teach them to remember the Christian way of firmness, of fairness; to set examples of Christ's teaching, such as, love one another even as I have loved you.

8. Pray in faith, believing. Know it is so as you believe.

The teacher seeks to fill a heart with love, with an understanding of God, and who knows, a mind steeped in God's Word, may sometime save a civilization, a country, a race.

Lord, Creator of us all,

We thank You for Your Word. We thank You for all the inspired teachers who have gone before us.

Open our minds to the wisdom You have given us through Your teachers who were inspired by Your Holy Spirit.

May we, using whatever talents You have given us, inspire the children to a reverence for Your Word. May we instill in them a faith to carry them through life.

May we too, live as examples of You, as Your children. Amen.

Spring Inspirations

21—Biblical Seeds In The Classroom

Isaiah 40:11: *"He shall feed his flock like a shepherd: he shall gather the lambs with his arm, and carry them in his bosom, and shall gently lead those that are with young."*
John 21:15: *"So when they dined, Jesus saith unto Simon Peter, son of Jonas, lovest thou me more than these? . . . He saith unto him, Feed my lambs."*
II Corinthians 9:10: *"Now he that ministereth seed to the sower both minister bread for your food, and multiply your seed sown, and increase the fruits of your righteousness."*

The students were seated according to size and according to physical and temperamental needs. Short students were seated in first rows, tall ones to the rear. Students with short attention spans or those with visual or hearing problems were given special front seats regardless of height.

Reading classes were formed to fit the needs of students. Slow or non-readers were together. Medium or grade-level readers formed another group, and the "zoomers" in still another.

I was dissatisfied with these arrangements. I began to look at the students as examples of well-known Biblical lessons. Two parables came to mind immediately—The Good Seed and The Lost Sheep.

It was easy to locate the good seeds—Susan and Joe. Their lessons were always completed on time. Homework came in neatly done and, of course, on time. They had fine relationships with parents, teachers, fellow-students. Their parents consulted Teacher regularly about their progress. But often they complained—these good seeds—"Teacher, what shall I do now?" How could I make better use of these good seeds so that they might produce an even better crop?

In our newspaper there appeared a story on the results of an experiment in New York schools. College students with below average grades were asked to tutor high school students who were underachieving. Results: the achievements of both college and high school students rose immediately.

In my classroom then, I made good seeds official helpers. Then the poor students clamored to be helpers. I had the impulse to refuse. But I remembered the newspaper story. I permitted poor students who had completed their work to help others still struggling. It worked, though in many cases it was like the blind leading the blind. But work improved on all levels.

Now to the lost sheep in the classroom.

Tommy was a loner, not only at school, but at home. He refused to join in games. At lunch hour he sat by himself, scarcely talking to his classmates. He sometimes wandered about the playground aimlessly. I tried in a roundabout way to find what interested him. But he couldn't or wouldn't say. My lost sheep who refused to be found!

Tommy's mother kept him in a Christian school, she often said, to get him out of the house early and return him home late. "I guess I just wasn't cut out to be a mother!" she often told me. Again, Jesus' admonition, "Feed my sheep," came to mind.

One day, Mr. Lusian, the caretaker, mentioned he certainly needed help with after-school cleaning. He was constantly late with lawn mowing, window cleaning and repairing. I was inspired to put two and two together—Mr. Lusian and his needs and Tommy with his. "Tommy is just a little boy, but why not try him?" I asked. It was agreed.

Tommy set to work, not as a loner, but with a man. He swept, he dusted. He mowed, he trimmed. He even displayed mechanical ability by repairing the mower when it refused to cut the grass evenly. Mr. Lusian paid him by the hour. Tommy repaid him by working harder and by confiding in his new companion his hopes and dreams. He wanted to be a caretaker for a church. "Then I can make things pretty for God."

Soon Tommy began communicating with me. He said, "I mow the lawn for Mom now. At first she said I'd be no good. But I told her I was helping Mr. Lusian. She wouldn't believe it at first!" he told me with enthusiasm. "And you know, I even wash a lot of my own clothes!"

And how his school work improved! Sometimes he even joined in games at recess. His happy smiles were miracles. That is, they might have been if I hadn't known the secret back of those smiles. Tommy had discovered he was a worthwhile person after all. Mr. Lusian had unknowingly followed Jesus' teaching: "Feed my sheep."

Dear Lord,

Help me to use my hands as He did.

Gently.

Help me to use my voice as He would want.

Gently.

Help me to use my mind and heart as though
They are true reflections of Him. Amen.

22—We Climbed the Mountain
For Jesus*

Job 32:8: *"But there is a spirit in man: and the inspiration of the Almighty giveth them understanding."*
II Timothy 3:15: *"And that from a child thou hast known the holy scriptures, which are able to make thee wise unto salvation through faith which is in Christ Jesus."*
II Timothy 3:16: *"All scripture is given by inspiration of God, and is profitable for doctrine, for reproof, for correction, for instruction in righteousness."*

Bible memory work in first grade at the Christian day school wasn't getting anywhere. Fridays, I assigned easy verses for homework: John 14:15 or Psalm 30:5 for beginning readers. The result? Mondays, instead of work accomplished, I got excuses. Magnificent excuses!

"My mother didn't have time to help me."

"We couldn't find that verse in our Bible."

"We went away for the weekend, and I didn't have time to study."

I tried teaching verses by rote in the classroom, but this was done at the expense of daily Bible lessons. What the children needed, I decided, was inspiration.

I rejected, in turn, stars on charts in compensation for verses learned, honor rolls, certificates, boy-versus-girl contests.

* Reprinted by permission of the American Sunday School Union.

Where one idea seemed trite, another was just uninspiring.

The newspaper carried a report about lost mountain climbers, and everyone in sharing time was excited that Monday when a boy described how his father had taken him part way up San Gorgonio, a nearby mountain the children knew well. "We got to a resting place, and we had lunch, then we climbed some more," Keith said breathlessly.

I noticed how wide-eyed the children were as they vicariously lived the adventure. My questing mind pounded on the idea. Why not climb a mountain for Jesus?

I secured a stand-up poster that our neighborhood druggist had discarded. Its dimensions (4' x 6') were just about right. Using brilliant poster paint, I made the sky blue, completing it with fluffy clouds. Then I painted in deep purples, greys and blacks, a rugged mountain topped with snow about two-thirds the poster's area. Into it I sketched ledges which would be resting places. These resting places were to indicate work accomplished. One, I labeled Psalm 23; another, five-verse point; another, Safety Ledge for Psalm 121. Circling the mountain's peak, I pasted a crown of gold stars.

Next, I cut strips of various colored construction paper (1" x 3"), and mounted on them colored pictures of boys and girls. I asked each child to print his own name on the strip marker of his own choice.

"What are we going to do, Teacher?" was the question I heard as we thumbtacked the strips to the base of the mountain on the bulletin board. The children had "oh-ed" and "ah-ed" over it since the moment of its appearance.

I explained we were going to do some mountain climbing for Jesus, that we were all going to start at the beginning—at the foot of the mountain—just as we all have equal chances to learn about Jesus.

"Some Christians grow in Him faster than others do. It all depends on how hard and how sincerely we work. I hope by year's end we'll all have safely reached a new way of thinking about the Christian life."

I explained further, "Each time a first grader completes a Bible memory verse, or an entire Psalm before the class without help, without mistakes, that child may move himself up to a named resting place." I added that the thumbtacks we were to think of as our minds, just as real mountain climbers use spikes and their knowledge of the mountain to help them reach the top.

I wasn't surprised, of course, when the quick students reached a resting place overnight. But to my vast relief, the slow ones quickly joined the fast ones. I heard no more excuses about no time, no help. No more, "Our Bible doesn't have that verse!"

Instead, they asked whether they might learn more verses, and so climb higher faster.

Bibles began appearing one by one. I heard more and more cries, "Teacher, help us find another verse. Please! I want to climb faster and reach the top first. Please, Teacher!"

I gave thanks. The Scripture was getting into their minds and so into my students' lives.

Dear Lord,

You have created us in Your own image. You have given us our lives to live in Your service. You have surrounded us with children waiting to be Inspired in Your service.

In these moments of meditation, we ask You to open our minds to new thoughts, to the welfare of the children in leading the Christian life.

Grant that we may find wisdom through Your holy Word to satisfy the needs of all we meet in our daily work.

For answering these requests, and for all blessings, we do give thanks. Amen.

23—The Children Taught Me!

Proverbs 14:33: *"Wisdom resteth in the heart of him that hath understanding."*
Proverbs 15:22: *"Without counsel purposes are disappointed: but in the multitude of counsellors they are established."*
I Corinthians 13:2: *"And though I have the gift of prophecy, and understand all mysteries, and all knowledge . . . so that I could remove mountains, and have not charity . . . it profiteth me nothing."*

During the time when I was learning to be cooperative with my students in third grade, I recalled the story of the little boy named David.

Constantly David was told, "You aren't being cooperative." His mother reminded him, "David, you aren't being cooperative with the family when you leave your clothes and toys scattered about." The father said, "David, you aren't being cooperative when you don't pull the weeds while I mow the lawn. You know I'm very busy." Little sister picked up the refrain. When David refused to let her play with his scooter, she complained, "Mother, David isn't being cooperative."

One night at prayer time, as he knelt beside his bed, David sobbed, "and dear God, can't they cooperate with me part of the time?"

Cooperation means interchange. It might mean joint ownership. It means doing things together. I learned to say, "Our books . . . Our lesson."

I was proud of the beautiful bulletin boards I created. *My* work! Or the work of superior students. One day a child asked, "How come, Teacher, you never put up any of my work? I'm here too." Show his inferior work? I had wanted visitors to see what a brilliant class I had. I prayed for forgiveness of my error and displayed all work. Who was I to judge anyway?

On another day I was dismayed at the sight of the cluttered room. Papers scattered here and there. A pencil lying in the aisle. I was tempted to say, "Children, your desks are a mess." But I looked at my own. It was anything but neat. I cleaned my desk and the children, following the example of their teacher, immediately began cleaning their own.

Later still, I was having problems with children who did not close their eyes during prayer time. Some of the open-eyed ones made faces at other open-eyed children. The result: giggling. I lost patience. "How can you pay attention to God if you are looking at someone and not thinking about Him?"

A child raised his hand. "Mrs. Vandermey, you didn't have your eyes shut either, or you wouldn't have seen Dick and Paul doing that!" I got the message! When the children finally realized Teacher was obeying her own orders, and trusting them, the students, prayer time became a time of quiet communication. All were cooperating because Teacher was cooperating.

During the year we undertook a difficult lesson project involving research in a number of library books. The children literally groaned at the enormity of the project. "All that work!" they cried.

"We'll cooperate," I said, using a lesson I'd learned from them.

The children divided the books. Each one looked up material for an assigned part. I looked up my part. We each chose one sentence and wrote it on the chalkboard. Then we rearranged them and the children copied them into their notebooks. Misspelled words were corrected. Result: the report was soon finished and no one complained. Not even the teacher! This cooperation method worked with the study of ants and it worked with learning about the states of the United States.

Cooperation—love in little things.

Heavenly Father,

Be with us this day in all our work.

Give us the insight into opportunities we have in the classroom to show loving Christian spirit.

Let us be tolerant of the whims of children.

Help us to be generous and understanding and so be an example for the children—kind, considerate.

We do give thanks for being present in our classrooms. Amen.

24—Love Is Like Sunlight

Ezekiel 17:8: *"It was planted in a good soil by great waters, that it might bring forth branches, and that it might bear fruit, that it might be a goodly vine."*
Proverbs 31:16: *"She considereth a field, and buyeth it: with the fruit of her hands she planteth a vineyard."*
Isaiah 44:3: *"For I will pour water upon him that is thirsty, and floods upon the dry ground: I will pour my spirit upon the seed, and my blessing upon thine offspring."*

Mrs. Roman, first grade teacher in a Christian day school, felt herself a close relative of a character in a popular play. "I must plant some seeds. I have nothing planted," he repeated and repeated.

Mrs. Roman.

Mrs. Roman continually doubted herself and her abilities. Naturally she wanted to serve God. But she continually asked herself, "Am I a good teacher? What if my principal or a parent came into my room now and found the children all talking at once? They should be quiet. Will I be blamed because I haven't been able to bring Andy up to grade level this year? I know they think he's superior. Why can't I make Connie read?"

Time went on and Mrs. Roman continued to feel the familiar frustration with herself. The familiar worry and concern became the thought pattern of her days. Then one night, her television screen jarred her loose from herself.

She sat late, watching a rerun of the Apollo 8 flight to the moon. She was breathless even though she knew the capsule would emerge from the dark side of the moon and would again be able to contact Ground Control at Houston. Would the great engine "burn"? The announcer gave the first telemetry readings, proof the capsule had indeed emerged. Now came the voice from outer space.

What were the first words spoken by those men in outer space? Did they say, "We're safe!" showing concern for only themselves? As humans, they must have felt relief. But the crew said no such thing. A strong clear voice came through for the world to hear. " . . . In the beginning God created the heaven and the earth. And the earth was without form, and void; and darkness was upon the face of the deep. And the Spirit of God moved upon the face of the waters. And God said, Let there be light: and there was light. . . ."

Mrs. Roman sat straight up. If those men thought more of God and His world at that dangerous time, than of themselves, how much more she could accomplish if she began thinking more about God's creation—the children—than of herself. Suppose she just let her faith and lovingness take over—Jesus saw the noisy children playing in the streets as blessed.

The teacher changed her behavior pattern. When a child became confused with a new step in modern math, she said patiently, "Let's do it together—God and you and me." She said to Connie, "God is helping me help you." She patted the child on the shoulder and praised her when she made even one small step ahead. She had planted the seed of confidence, of accomplishment.

The new thought patterns did not come easily, for the habit of self-concern was strong. But the rewards finally came. As the teacher's self-concern weakened, her other-person concern strengthened. She *felt* God guiding her. She felt elation when Andy's fist thumped on his desk, and he yelled, "I get'cha, Teacher!" And Connie said quietly, "I see it now. It's easy." The seeds were beginning to grow.

A child spilled his carton of milk at lunchtime one day. Without condemnation Mrs. Roman sponged up the milk while the child drew back, expecting punishment. She whispered, "Is is all right, Teacher?"

Mrs. Roman replied, "Of course. It was an accident." God

made little children that way. Their muscles had not yet developed. It was up to adults to understand this. This teacher was now giving of her lovingness. A current of goodwill flowed between teacher and student. Both were blessed.

In recognition of her newly-acquired love-giving, her understanding of self and the other person, Mrs. Roman's prayers began to change. She asked less for herself, more for the children of her class, even as Commander Borman's Bible reading was more in praise of God than of himself and his companions.

Mrs. Roman now felt herself as the planter of seeds in the children, seeds of self-confidence, of accomplishment, of self-acceptance. It was her duty and privilege to expose those seeds to the sunlight of the Heavenly Father's love that was in her.

The seeds would grow and mature as God intended.

Oh, God,

Give us the vision of Your care for the children in our care. Grant to each child the knowledge that he can be Your child through faith in Jesus.

Open our minds to Your goodness, Your greatness, that we may bring peace and harmony in our part of the world.

Help us to think less of ourselves and more of others. Give us the patience and understanding we need in helping the Andys, the Connies of our classes.

For the blessings You shower upon us, for the opportunities to serve, we do give thanks. Amen.

25—Hurry! The Flower Will Die!

Ecclesiastes 3:11: *"He hath made every thing beautiful in his time: also he hath set the world in their heart, so that no man can find out the work that God maketh from the beginning to the end."*
Psalm 90:17: *"And let the beauty of the Lord our God be upon us: and establish thou the work of our hands upon us; yea, the work of our hands establish thou it."*
Romans 12:10: *"Be kindly affectioned one to another with brotherly love; in honour preferring one another."*

Joey came into our third grade room late as usual. As usual, too, his face was streaked with mud, his jeans coated with it. I knew what had happened on the way to school. He had taken advantage of the mud puddles along the way and stopped to build a dam across the tiny stream in the street. He couldn't resist.

As usual, too, he slammed the door behind him, causing the girls to jump. He made as much noise as possible clumping along the aisle, bumping desks. At the cloak closet he turned and grinned at me, showing wide gaps in his mouth where two teeth were missing. *Is she going to read the riot act to me?* I knew he was wondering.

I didn't smile back. I motioned for him to be quiet, not to disturb the class. But he slammed the closet door and clumped down the aisle to his seat, still grinning. It was a losing battle with my patience. "Joey, you're disturbing the class!"

"Yeah," said Patti. "He likes to mess up everything!"

Joey put his head down on his desk and Tim said, "Now, look what you've done! You made him cry!"

"Class!" I ordered. "Quiet. Please continue with your math!"

What could I do? Any attempt I'd made in these first months of the school year to communicate with Joey made him withdraw. I felt he resented me close to him. "Patience, Lord. Give me patience. I love him, can't he see that? Doesn't he know what a disturbance he is?" I prayed. Joey needed help.

His father had deserted, and his mother was just too busy with new friends to bother with him. She had enrolled him in our Christian school, she said, because, "I want him to be Christian." The paternal grandmother kept him weekends, washed and mended his clothing. Joe needed love, but he refused it. Besides, I couldn't condemn him for his love of mud. Hadn't I as a child loved to run in the rain, splashing through water? And what good was a tree with its rough bark which skinned my knees, except for climbing? "Learn to be a lady!" my own grandmother had ordered. But the orders went in one ear and out the other. Yes, Joey, I mused, I know how you feel. But you must not disturb this class!

No admonitions prevented his disturbing the class, not even staying in at recess to contemplate his rule-breaking. The other children refused to play with him, but he did not change. I loved him for many reasons: I identified with him. He had a grandmother who "only did her duty!" He, too, loved mud and rain. I loved him because God had sent him to me. But—there remained that but.

At recess one cold rainy day, I stood at the door while the children left for drinks at the fountain and trips to the washrooms. Joey passed me. He had just knocked down Susan. I was prepared to stop him for yet another admonition and perhaps to deny him even a few minutes freedom, when I noticed his sweater hanging loose. "Button your sweater, Joey," I said. "You'll freeze."

"It ain't got no buttons. Grandma ain't. . . ." He stopped.

"Wait, I'll fix it." I brought out safety pins from my desk drawer and fastened the much worn sweater.

He didn't thank me, just looked at me, his blue eyes wide and suddenly damp. Then he skipped happily to the drinking fountain. The first show of joy I'd ever seen in him.

When he returned he was still in the happy mood. I pulled him close to me. He responded for just a second, letting his head rest against me, then, self-conscious, he went to his desk and put his head down. Was he crying? I dared not approach him. He wouldn't want attention drawn to him.

Next morning at faculty devotions, Joey's face appeared at the office window. He rapped on the glass. I motioned for him to leave as we were having Bible reading. The other teachers stirred impatiently at the intrusion into our quiet minutes.

But he persisted. Would he never learn? I'd repeatedly warned the children against this kind of interruption.

At last he pounded on the door. Frowning, I opened it, prepared to remind him once more not to disturb the teachers at devotions.

But my admonitions were trapped in my throat. Joey was holding a bright red morning glory out to me. "Here, Teacher," he said. "I have to give it to you in a hurry. It will die in a minute. It's to tell you I love you too."

I was overwhelmed, confused. He loved me, but had been afraid before this to show it. Joey wanted and needed attention that is given out of love. He was giving me this short-lived flower to show his love.

Jesus said we must love one another. But there is a time limit. We must make the most of the moment which presents itself for showing our concern for a fellow man, for helping him, for sharing our love. But Jesus gave no condition of value—just love. What Joey needed was someone who loved him for himself, not because of duty.

"Thank you, Joey," I said. "I love you too." I tucked the already wilting morning glory into the buttonhole of my sweater.

Joey smiled, then ran. We had a beginning. Love had paved the way to develop his possibilities. I knew he would be a different boy from now on.

Dear Lord,

Remind us we have been placed in the orbit of each child's existence for a purpose.

Remind us, Lord, what we say, what we do, how we react to each situation in our contacts with the children will affect them for good, or for bad. May our efforts be Your way.

May we always be direct channels to Your wisdom as we speak, as we plan, and as we teach.

For Your responses through us, we give thanks. Amen.

26—The Mustard Seed Child

Isaiah 41:10: *"Fear thou not; for I am with thee: be not dismayed; for I am thy God: I will strengthen thee; yea, I will help thee; yea, I will uphold thee with the right hand of my righteousness."*
Matthew 6:30: *"Wherefore, if God so clothe the grass of the field, which to day is, and to morrow is cast into the oven, shall he not much more clothe you, O ye of little faith?"*

"Dear Lord," I prayed daily in the California desert community where I had arrived a month earlier to make my home, "I know you called me to teach Your children. You know my needs. But there is no place for me here. You promised to help me. But how? There's no job for me."

I told my neighbor of my problem. Her daughter Cindy attended a Christian day school. But she knew of no openings. I began to feel I'd made a wrong move from a major metropolis to this small community.

One morning my phone rang. The secretary of the school Cindy was attending was calling. "We need someone to supervise lunch hour," she said. "Our Mrs. Norris is ill."

I, a trained, experienced teacher reduced to lunch-hour duty? Momentarily my false pride stopped me, but only momentarily.

As I worked at the lunch tables, opening milk cartons, wiping up spills, I confess to some envious minutes as the teachers went to their lunchroom, chatting, no doubt, about events of the morning's school work. Determinedly, I said, "Thanks, anyway, Lord, for this opportunity!"

I discovered I was smiling as the children told me about their pet turtles, dogs, cats and snakes. Then we moved onto the playground.

How familiar it was! The slides, monkey bars, an improvised baseball diamond on the field which had been plowed to rid it of weeds, a constant fire hazard in desert communities. Nevertheless, tufts of mustard plants and sunflowers, determined to live in spite of the plow, dotted the area.

Some children began racing toward me. One little girl, clutching a handful of mustard flowers, those determined weeds of the desert, broke ahead and reached me first. Though we were virtually strangers, there she stood before me, blond hair flying, blue eyes shining in perfect trust. "They're for you!" she cried, and without waiting for my "Thank you!" she raced away. Other children, aware now of my ready acceptance of the flowers, brought me more.

But now, noon hour was over. I'd enjoyed myself so much I couldn't accept the pay offered me though I certainly could have used it.

At home, I placed the mustard flowers in my best vase and placed them on a table where the afternoon sunlight touched them and bounced off to fill the room with golden beauty.

The flowers wilted and died. I delayed throwing them away, wanting to hold on to the love of the children they represented. I noticed some little seed pods where the flowers had been. Carefully I broke off one, cracked it open. There lay the tiny seed, so small I could never have found it if I were to drop it on the carpet.

Holding it in my hand, I pictured the naked field where it had survived. I remembered the plants growing, branching out in all directions, putting out blooms in spite of heat and lack of water. They were full of the creative force of God.

Had the seed in the earth tossed and turned and worried, "I'm small, I have no water, just heat? Am I ever going to grow?" Of course it hadn't. It had just lain there, drinking in the scant rain when it came, knowing all the while it would live and produce.

For the first time I knew the real message to us of the Bible verse, "If you have the faith of a grain of mustard seed. . . ." I relaxed, let go of my worry over lack of work. I became a human mustard seed. God knew what was best for me. I felt at home for the first time in Rio Oro.

In church that Sunday, even the minister in his message seemed to know my situation, for he said in part, "It's God's will that you have everything you need. He blesses you when you accept Him and His gifts. 'If therefore thine eye be single, thy whole body shall be full of light' (Matthew 6:22)." As I left the church I saw the little mustard-seed girl. She rushed up and hugged me around the knees.

Later, however, in the continued waiting, my mind rebelled. I felt so powerless, my faith wavered. But wait, I reminded myself, remember the mustard seed. No tossing, no turning. Just pray and wait. So I did.

The waiting in faith paid off. The secretary of the school where I'd filled in for lunch duty called. "Our Mrs. Jory of first grade is going to have a baby and must take time off. Will you fill in for her? The children adored you."

Would I? And I'd be the teacher of the mustard-seed girl.

Now, because Mrs. Jory decided to remain at home to care for her baby, I was in the classroom on a permanent basis—where God planned for me to be all along. The mustard seed that is me is growing into a plant in full bloom.

Loving God,

As we stop our activities for these moments to talk with You, we ask You to give us open minds, ready to receive fresh knowledge of You. Open our ears that through the laughter of children we can hear Your voice.

Give us open eyes that we may be more alert to the beauties of the world You made. Give us open hands ready to help all those who may need us this day.

For all blessings, and trials of our lives too, we give thanks. We know the trials are ours so that we may grow in faith, in love, in patience. Amen.

27—Tension Breakers

Psalm 85:8: *"I will hear what God the Lord will speak: for he will speak peace unto his people, and to his saints: but let them not turn again to folly."*
Isaiah 26:3: *"Thou wilt keep him in perfect peace, whose mind is stayed on thee: because he trusteth in thee."*
John 14:27: *"Peace I leave with you, my peace I give unto you: not as the world giveth, give I unto you. Let not your heart be troubled, neither let it be afraid."*

A mother came into the first grade schoolroom just as the day's session was about to begin. She gave the teacher a bottle of pills—tranquilizers—for her son John. "I don't like to impose. I know you're busy. But will you give John one each noon. If you don't, he'll be climbing the walls afternoons. Be sure he swallows the pill. Sometimes. . . ."

The teacher sighed. Yesterday Jeannie's mother had brought another prescription and had given it to the teacher with explicit instructions for administering the medication to her daughter. The teacher began to feel tension building within her. Laughingly she showed the first bottle to John's mother. "I wonder what would happen if I'd begin taking those medications too."

The horrified mother exclaimed, "Oh, you mustn't! No telling what would happen!"

Of course the teacher was joking, and also trying to relieve tension.

What can the Christian teacher do to relax tense nerves which develop as a result of association with noisy children, and even from the plain activity-noise of a busy classroom? How can a teacher remain calm and collected when one problem has gone out the back door, as two more enter the front? Children argue over the possession of a pencil. An unhappy mother spills her home problems to Teacher. A visitor, wondering whether or not to enroll her child in the class, sits in the back of the room taking notes while Teacher attempts to conduct business as usual.

That the Christian teacher prays for patience, for understanding, for serenity in the face of turmoil goes without saying. But God expects a teacher to use the brain which He gave her too.

In a first grade room, a new teacher discovered a woolly lamb with a built-on music box. The toy, once white, was a grimy, fuzzy gray from long, hard usage. The only tune it played was "Rock-a-Bye Baby." She inquired about trying to find the owner. But no one claimed it. She left it on the reading table. The children called it Baa-Baa.

One day, the teacher felt her patience with a room full of noisy children reaching the snapping point. In desperation, after stern reminders to the children to quiet down, she walked to the reading table to straighten the books. Anything to gain time. "I must get hold of myself," she thought. She picked up the lamb and set it to the back of the table. The toy began to tinkle out an unplayed part of the tune "Rock-a-Bye Baby."

The buzz and confusion in the room stopped as the children listened to the gentle song. Peace came into the room. All worked quietly at their papers. "That was nice, Teacher," one child said. "Play it again." The teacher wound up the lamb, and the children listened as they worked.

After that, when the noise reached a pitch which even troubled some child, he (she) would tip-toe to the table, pick up the lamb, wind it, set it down, and the song would begin again. "I wouldn't lose that lamb for a month's salary," the teacher said later. "It even makes me feel relaxed." For a change in melody, she purchased some records of gentle songs to play while the children were doing arithmetic bookwork.

One day, another teacher was trying to draw from the students examples of how they worked off tension. George spoke up. "When I go home and feel kinda mad, I go to the frig and get some celery. I chew out as hard as I can on anything I'm mad at."

"But we sure can't chew celery in school!" objected another child.

"We play hard games at recess. That sure helps," said Kathie.

A teacher in third grade, in imitation of the use of the peace sign, held up her fingers when noise mounted and the children seemed tense, uncooperative. This appealed to the children's sense of humor. They too held up their fingers. Tension eased. Quiet prevailed.

Patience, ingenuity, these are the self-administered anaesthetics which hold minds motionless while the Father seeks to restore minds to tranquility. Then the work in the classroom progresses according to schedule.

Dear Lord,

We thank You for the love of You which follows us daily. We thank You for informing our minds of ways in which to seek peace. We thank You for every evidence of Your Spirit's leading us into paths of tranquility.

May our minds and hearts be ever ready and open to receive Your messages even though it may be only through a ragged and woolly lamb. For all blessings You so freely give, we offer thanks. Amen.

28—Do You Mean Me?*

Proverbs 31:20: *"She stretcheth forth her hand to the poor; yea, she reacheth forth her hands to the needy."*
John 14:18: *"I will not leave you comfortless: I will come to you."*

For weeks, I had tried with Becky, a shy, frightened black girl who had recently enrolled. Becky was a fine student, but at recesses, she kept to herself, swinging round and round on the swing supports aimlessly. When I tried to draw her into games, she would say, "I don't feel so good today." She even refused to be messenger, a task of distinct honor for other students.

I realized she must feel alone as the only "different" child in a group of two hundred. But if I pushed too hard I knew she would catch on to my purpose. With a deepening sense of failure, I watched her swinging forlornly. I remembered a beloved Bible quotation, "I will not leave you comfortless: I will come to you" (John 14:18). God's promise. I prayed for wisdom. I prayed for a way to help Becky. I knew I was not alone in the situation; I knew help was available. I relaxed, knowing the answer would come.

One day, however, I received a note from the distraught mother of Sharon.

Dear Mrs. Vandermey, will you please give Sharon

* From *Evangel*, January 1968, used by permission of Light and Life Press.

extra attention this week? Her daddy has gone away. She
is heartbroken for he was very dear to her. She doesn't
understand why he deserted us. And I don't either.

Sharon was an only child, her mother a teacher in another
school. Sharon too was a loner, with few friends. She, like
Becky, resented my attempts to help her integrate into a
world she was rejecting. Again, I needed to push without
showing it.

The problem churned in my mind. Though I praised
Sharon for her good work, she never smiled in response.
Several times she put her head down on her desk, and always
some alert child reported, "Teacher, Sharon's crying."

I knew I needed to do some more praying. And I did,
earnestly. I knew somehow the Lord would point the way.

So it went for several days. One Wednesday at recess I
watched Sharon, alone, staring at the grass. As usual, Becky
was alone on the steps. Two lonely upset girls. I, their helpless
teacher.

I sat down beside Becky. "Becky," I said quietly and
confidingly, "Sharon's father has gone away. She's lonesome
for him. You have so much she doesn't have. A mother *and* a
daddy. Will you help me help her? Go ask her to help you
make up some counting rhymes. Maybe you can help her
more than I can." I was breathless, even as I prayed this might
be the solution.

The small dark face with the deep brown eyes turned
toward me. Tears came. A look of wonderment crossed her
face, but then she seemed to shrivel into her usual lonely self.

"Me, I couldn't help anybody."

I had caught that single glimmer of interest. I went on,
"Sharon hurts terribly inside. Maybe you know how it feels to
hurt. . . ."

The tears spilled down her face. "Yes, I do. I hurt inside and
outside all the time." She jabbed at her tears. "I'm different."

"If you hurt that way, then you must know how Sharon
feels. Let's pray together for her. I don't mean out loud, but
just inside ourselves. God will hear our thoughts. He answers
prayers. He knows we need His help."

I closed my eyes, hoping she would do the same.

Soon, rubbing her hands together nervously, she stood up. I
touched her shoulder encouragingly. She walked away, but

stayed by herself. Was she going to help Sharon? "Lord, I've planted the seed. I believe You guided me. Now, Lord, it's up to You!" The prayer lifted the cloud over me.

I wandered across the playground, not glancing toward Becky or Sharon. Soon I heard soft, almost silky, laughter. I turned. Becky, Sharon and Millie were jumping rope. I knew I'd be forgiven for prolonging recess five minutes.

When I rang the bell, there was the usual rush to hold Teacher's hand, the children declaring, "We're stuck on Teacher!" This day was special, for Becky reached me first, then Sharon, making fumbling attempts to communicate. Becky was laughing. It was a day to remember.

The change, dramatic as it was that day, had its ups and downs. But Becky finally assumed, then accepted, rightful membership in the school. She and Sharon became good friends.

As the good friends developed into a best friends situation, I became increasingly aware of a basic truth of our Christian life. To have a feeling of being needed, and to be able to satisfy that need, is one of our richest blessings, even in third grade. We had followed the admonition: help one another.

Gracious Father,

Let me hear Your voice today. Touch my mind so that I may know what You would have me do in my classroom. May my knowledge of You give me more understanding, more Christian love in helping my students with their problems.

Open my mental ears so that I may always hear the silent pleas for help of each child.

Teach me to answer in complete understanding when one says, "Teacher, I'm scared . . . Teacher, I don't belong . . . I'm worried."

Thank You for giving me the opportunity of Christian service. Amen.

29—Boy In Sugar

Proverbs 14:26: *"In the fear of the Lord is strong confidence: and his children shall have a place of refuge."*
Matthew 9:36: *"But when he saw the multitudes, he was moved with compassion on them, because they fainted, and were scattered abroad, as sheep having no shepherd."*

Frantic knocks at the door of our third grade class startled us. We had just finished roll call, flag salutes, and Bible lesson. Connie, official hostess, jumped up to perform her duties. As she opened the door, loud sobbing sounds interrupted our activities.

Connie returned and whispered, "It's an old lady. She's crying, Teacher."

Asking the children to busy themselves with silent reading, I went outside.

A heavy-set woman in her seventies stood waiting, dabbing her eyes with a soggy tissue. "I'm Joe's grandmother," she sobbed. "He's out there in the car. He won't come in. He wants to stay with me."

Joe, again. Joe who never did his homework, who never learned his spelling words. Joe, who had no friends.

"I'll try to pursuade him to come," I told the grandmother as we started for the parking lot. Descending the steps, she groaned, her tears beginning again. "My arthritis is so bad I just can't take these steps. I can't take those children either. But I love them. They need me."

I helped her as best I could.

I knew the background of the family. The father worked far away from home. The mother was attending college, working toward a degree, leaving the children alone nights until late. She reminded me of Rousseau, of whom it was said, he had so much fun writing about education that he put his children in an orphanage while he wrote about it.

I could hear Joe crying, but where was he? "He's sure here somewhere," the grandmother said.

Joe was hiding under the instrument panel. A ten-pound bag of sugar the grandmother had evidently purchased on the way to school had fallen off the seat, breaking, and Joe was sitting in it. I opened the car door, touching him gently. "Joe, it's time for school."

He only cried harder.

"They took his mother to the hospital yesterday," the grandmother explained. "Nobody told me till today. She just had an upset from examinations. Last night a neighbor caught Joe setting a brushfire. She called me and I got the kids. If only my son would get a job here, or take his family with him."

Joe refused to leave the car with gentle persuasion. I had to use the stronger kind. "Come, Joe." I seized his arms and hauled him out. Sugar came along, spilling onto the blacktop.

Now they both cried harder. But she quickly drove away. Joe, twisted around, crying, "'Bye, Grandma!" The despair in his voice left me emotionally in shreds.

Now I was left with Joe, coated with sugar. Could I take him into the classroom where he would be the target of thirty pairs of curious and perhaps derisive eyes? As we neared the door, he tried to struggle free. "I won't go in!"

Of course not! "Joe, go wash your face and dust off your clothes. Stay awhile, then come back. I won't tell the class."

He stumbled away. Suppose he ran? I hoped he would not. What was happening to my unattended class? I hurried inside.

To my relief the room was quiet. The children were playing a favorite trick on Teacher. Every head was down on a desk, mischievous eyes peeking through fingers at me.

"Thank you, Class!" I said happily.

Everyone, grinning, accepted the assignment for reading. But my mind was on Joe. The little boy in sugar, as I named him mentally, needed help. I wanted him to do well in school.

I wanted him to have friends. But as one teacher said, "Some children are more easily loved than others." Joe was one of the others.

What to do? I found an idea.

Each year in our grade, we organized a secret Christian Service club. Each member performed some act of Christian kindness each week, and prayed for anyone needing help. Fridays, we told what we had done. We never bragged. We never expected nor accepted rewards. Since children love secrets, no one ever told the details, just what they had done. Why, I asked myself now, couldn't the class help Joe? Could they be relied upon not to make their help obvious? I had to take a chance.

I called a halt to study. I had to move quickly because Joe might appear (but then, he might have run away!). I explained Joe's mother was sick, that his daddy was away, and now Joe needed us. Why not make it a club project to help him—in secret of course. Jesus helped people. We could try to follow His example.

Time ran out. The door opened. Joe came in, slid into his seat. To my relief, only a few curious glances went his way.

One boy began to work on Joe immediately. "Teacher, kin—I mean may I help Joe with arithmetic?" Such a request was common enough. At recess Tom said he didn't feel like playing kickball, and could he and Joe just swing? As the day went on, more and more children paid Joe special attention. I prayed earnestly, "God, don't let them overdo it!" The prayer was answered in a reverse way. Joe simply blossomed.

Joe was among the several children required to stay in last recess to complete spelling word practice long overdue. All except Joe finished and left. I glanced over his page, checking the sentences using spelling words. One of the words was "lose!" He had written, "I am going to lose my mother." The sheet trembled in my hand.

After consultation with my principal, we decided a call on the mother was necessary. We telephoned and made an appointment.

A tall, thin woman in her late twenties greeted us, then shooed Joe outside. He resisted, but I assured him he had nothing to be afraid about. Reluctantly he left.

The mother said, "I've only two years to go before I get my degree." She pushed nervous hands together.

"But the children need you," I said quietly. All the while I was thinking, "Don't condemn. Jesus didn't!" I gave her Joe's spelling lesson.

She read it. When she saw the sentence, "I'm going to lose my mother," she began crying. "I didn't know! I'll try harder."

"Joe needs assurance you care," I said gently.

"I'll try harder," she repeated. Did she mean she would postpone her college work? I didn't know.

But now, as time went on, Joe improved in mental outlook. The class continued to "work on him" and he blossomed under the warmth of attention. Wasn't it Luther Burbank who said, "Every weed can be transformed into a flower"?

True, Joe didn't set any scholastic records, but he tried. Even as host for the week, he surprised me with his friendly manners in greeting guests.

One day he appeared with a foil-wrapped package. He said proudly, "My mother baked these cookies for our class. Kin I pass them at lunchtime, Teacher?"

I thanked the Heavenly Father right then and there. Joe's mother was answering the call of duty, through love. Joe did his homework and on time. Joe was no longer late for school. Joe was being loved at home and at school. He was returning love according to his feelings.

When he said to me one day, "Teacher, every day now, I feel like a different person," I knew exactly what he meant. He was a little boy in sugar, and I didn't mean the kind that comes in bags. Christian Service Club had worked. We had applied the principles of Christ's teaching.

Lord,

Today we stand in the light of Your divine knowledge.

Let us recognize the needs of each student in our charge. Give us wisdom, courage, to help fulfill those needs.

Without the inspiration of Your holy Word, we feel helpless.

Thank You for instilling love for little children in us and for putting love in the hearts of little children for each other. Amen.

30—Teacher, Nobody's Perfect*

Proverbs 1:5: *"A wise man will hear, and will increase learning; and a man of understanding shall attain unto wise counsels."*
Proverbs 4:5: *"Get wisdom, get understanding: forget it not; neither decline from the words of my mouth."*
Romans 3:23: *"For all have sinned, and come short of the glory of God."*

One day, I learned my students expected me to know everything. Francis held up his hand for recognition. "What is it, Francis?" I asked.

"Teacher, what is the temperature of the sun?"

I was honest about it. "I don't know. Let's look it up in the science book."

"Some teacher!" I heard him mutter. "Doesn't know *that!*"

I wanted to shake him, for I felt humiliated. I wanted so to be perfect. My day was ruined. But that night, I did some self-examination. Why should I have felt that way? A child, undeveloped, has not yet learned the art of subtlety. If he wants to know, he wants to know. Teacher is supposed to be able to tell him on the spot. But there was more to it than that. I wanted to be perfect. I must excel. I had a false pride.

I went back in time to my childhood. If I did not keep up with my brother (and I seldom did), my parents asked, "Why

* Revised from *Home Life*, September 1976. Copyright ® 1976 by The Sunday School Board of the Southern Baptist Convention. All rights reserved. Used by permission.

can't you be as smart as Allen?" There were worse things to come. I was told, "You'll never need an education anyway. Your brother is going to be a minister. You'll just get married." So I worked harder, I had to over-achieve in order to survive emotionally, though in my childish thoughts it amounted to trying to surpass Allen.

Now, in my schoolroom, I understood myself somewhat better. I must not demand perfection from myself nor from my children.

In spite of my intentions, I told Joe one day, "Joe, you didn't do this arithmetic as you should. You can do better."

"Well, Teacher," he replied, "nobody's perfect!"

I learned my own lesson.

So, eventually, with prayer, I set up some guidelines (a course of study) for myself:

1. I will remember to ask myself: Why do I want to coddle this child? Why do I want to be stern with that one?
2. I will remember the saying, "Until I walk a mile in the other man's shoes, I cannot know his problems."
3. I will remember to confide in parents occasionally. It helps to share.
4. There is *no* normal way. There are only separate trails leading to one goal—the child's ultimate good. Hopefully the trails will converge. The child will grow to adulthood with healthy attitudes, be emotionally strong and academically able, and have a sturdy Christian faith.

Ever-present Lord,

Help us to willingly, humbly admit our wrongs. Let us be such good examples of Your teachings to our charges that they may learn humility as well as the joyousness which comes from admissions of our wrongs, not only to ourselves, but to others.

Help the children to know, having learned from their teachers, the good feeling of honesty.

Help us, Lord, to understand and forgive the weaknesses in others as we would have them understand and forgive us.

Thank You for the privilege of being able to come to You in prayer, knowing You are always ready to strengthen and help us. Amen.

Final Weeks

31—Take Your Children
On Wonder Walks

Genesis 1:21: *"And God created great whales, and every living creature that moveth, which the waters brought forth abundantly, after their kind, and every winged fowl after his kind: and God saw that it was good."*

Psalm 111:3,4: *"His work is honourable and glorious: and his righteousness endureth for ever. He hath made his wonderful works to be remembered: the Lord is gracious and full of compassion."*

A mother in a supermarket with her four-year-old was hurriedly selecting groceries. But the child stooped to examine the unbelievably red colors on tomato cans. She cried, "Dodie, why must you dawdle?"

The child protested, "I want to see!"

A little child knows life is good and beautiful, and he approaches the tangibles of living as though they never present problems. The so-called commonplace is miraculous. In his small mind, he sees a pyramid in an ant hill.

How can the busy teacher take the children on wonder walks, even though there scarcely seems time for academics?

A second grade teacher's reading class was interrupted when a child discovered a small spider spinning a web from the ceiling. A girl grabbed a notebook with which to sweep the creature away. "Wait, Judy," the teacher said, "let's watch the spider. It won't harm us."

Reading forgotten, the children gathered to watch. The teacher explained, "Watch the spider spinning the web from its own body. It's being guided by something it probably doesn't even understand."

"When the spider spins a web how does it know when to turn the corners?" Andy asked.

"Its Creator—God—put the knowing into him," the teacher replied. "The material comes out of its body to make the web as strong as steel wire about the same size (meaning tensile strength). And God tells the spider when to turn corners."

The children gasped. Unknowingly, they had been on a wonder walk.

The teacher continued, "If these creatures don't endanger our lives, we leave them alone, or we gently put them outside. Not let's wait until the spider reaches the floor, then we'll slip a paper under him and take the creature outside where he belongs."

One of the brave boys performed the service.

Watch a child alone. He will see a minute creature and stoop to watch it, perhaps poke it with a wary toe, instinctively wondering about it. If the teacher hurries him away, an instinctive bent for investigation may be stifled.

One first grade teacher took the class on weekly wonder walks. With a stick they marked off one-foot squares in patches of grass. On their knees, the children examined their own spots in detail. What did they see?

"I see little rocks. Blue ones, green ones, white ones. . . ." "I see a spider. . . ." "I see a green bug. . . ." "I see a red bug. . . ." "I see a worm poking its head up through a hole. . . ." "I see. . . ."

Later, the teacher tabulated the results of the wonder walk on the chalkboard as the children remembered and reported. One day they had seen fifty different kinds of animal life and twelve colors of stones. And they had examined many varieties of plant life, each from the child's own plot of ground.

Permitting a child free expression of his instinct for joy and utilizing his naturalness can encourage his inspiration.

Teacher Arlene Wilson reported this incident. "My first floor apartment is on the route to a near-by elementary school. My breakfast table view reaches across a vacant lot to the mountains beyond. Mornings I watch mothers taking their little ones to school. Some drag their little ones along. But not so one mother on a dark rainy morning.

"As the mother and child were passing my window, a streak of sunlight broke through the clouds and touched the weeds and grass ahead of them. The scene changed. The cone of sunlight turned dead plants to red, gold, green and blue. A flock of blackbirds swooped down, settled in the shaft of sunlight. The child broke away from his mother and ran to the shaft of sun, scattering the protesting birds.

"The father, accompanied by a mud-coated white poodle now came along, and the dog joined the child. Both mother and father, caught up in the magic moment, joined boy and dog. Parents, child joined hands and they danced round and round laughing with joy.

"A rainbow appeared over the mountains. Its arc of colors reached from peak to peak. The father pointed to the rainbow and all three faces were illumined with the beauty of God's creation. There can be no doubt that later in life, in some remote place, the child, become a man, will recall the morning his parents took time to join him in that wonder experience. He will remember with gratefulness.

"Those parents, of course, will never know how they inspired me," concluded Arlene Wilson. "Since then, I've always taken time from schoolwork to stop and permit the children of the classroom to appreciate some manifestation of God's creation. A cloud castle over the mountains; birds building nests under the eaves; a harmless bug lost on our schoolroom floor. The children, refreshed by this time of wonder, happily return to their books."

Dear Lord,

We ask You to help us remember to slow our pace, to open our eyes to the beauties of Your creation.

Help us to see Your handiwork as it is presented to us—cloud castle, a bird, a bug, a blade of grass. In our hurry to learn from books, we too often overlook the special things You have created.

As we pause in this quiet time of day, we thank You for

all the beauties of Your world. And in this pause, we find refreshment and peace. Amen.

32—God's Grace

Psalm 51:10: *"Create in me a clean heart, O God; and renew a right spirit within me."*
Isaiah 57:19: *"I create the fruit of the lips; Peace, peace to him that is far off, and to him that is near, saith the Lord; and I will heal him."*
Romans 1:17: *"For therein is the righteousness of God revealed from faith to faith: as it is written, The just shall live by faith."*

In regularly scheduled self-evaluation meetings, we teachers discussed ways we might become better Christians. We all agreed the sharing of problems helped. We came away from the meetings comforted, uplifted, knowing we were all in the process of "becoming" effective followers of the Lord and Master Teacher.

At our meetings, second grade teacher Carol listened intently, but she did not participate. She seemed remote, encased within herself.

This was Carol's first year of teaching. She was about twenty-five, a small, bright-haired person, a stranger in our small community. We teachers knew Principal Farley spent much time with her, counseling her after complaints from parents.

Carol, it was rumored, was short-tempered, even occasionally harsh as a teacher. She seldom smiled. She had a locked-in look. She taught as though she feared giving of herself. "Isn't she a Christian?" one parent asked. "What's wrong with her?" asked another.

The children were the loudest in their complaints: "Miss Moresby isn't fair! Miss Moresby won't. . . ."

Carol confided in no one, associated with no one. Oh, she was polite—rigidly polite. She lived alone in a small apartment and was seldom seen outside school hours. All the teachers, at one time or another, had asked her to spend Saturday or Sunday evening with them. With a faint, yet somehow regretful smile, she had refused.

But one morning at the end of the school year when we assembled for our self-evaluation meeting, we were in for a surprise. After the usual Bible reading, Mr. Farley announced, "We'll dispense with our usual discussion today. Carol wants to tell us something." Carol *asking* to speak!

There was something different about her this day. She seemed relaxed, at peace with herself. She leaned forward, elbows on the table, and held her hands together as though in prayer. The rest of us seemed to be holding our collective breath.

She began, "I had an experience this past weekend I want to share. I know you're all surprised that at last I'm speaking in one of these meetings. I—I—just couldn't before. But first I want to thank you all for being so kind to me this year. I didn't deserve it . . ." Her voice broke and tears glistened in her eyes.

"I deliberately isolated myself. I'd moved a thousand miles to get away from home, from my family. . . ." She fought for control. "I never wanted to see them again. I was hurt, terribly hurt. . . . I can't tell you why. Yet. Maybe I can some day. But I couldn't forgive them. And the more I felt I couldn't forgive them, the more I couldn't forgive myself. I really didn't feel worthy, yet I kept trying, trying.

"Last week was critical. My parents wrote, asking me to come home. I couldn't, just couldn't. I couldn't forgive them. I felt so miserable, so desperate, I went for a walk even while it was raining. I went along the arroyo beside the row of eucalyptus trees. Those trees are new to me. We don't have them back—back home. I stopped to examine them—how they're always shedding their bark, how clean and smooth the trunks are when the bark has dropped away. I picked up a strip of bark, out of curiosity, I suppose. I walked onto the bridge and stood in the center and looked down at the swirling water.

"I watched that water, swirling about, carrying debris with it. Why, I can't explain, I began breaking off pieces of bark and letting them drop into the water. I watched each piece as it was carried away and put of sight. I dropped another . . . another. . . ." She choked with emotion, gained control and went on. "Something was happening to me. I'm sure God was touching me, guiding me. I literally felt pieces of me dropping away. By pieces I mean something I couldn't touch. Minute by minute I began to feel different. Finally I knew what the pieces were. The bark, floating away, represented the hate, the pretense I'd been living in. I realized this—all this—was what had been making me act the way I did. I rejected you. I rejected my children. I envied everyone for having happy homes. Loved ones. Suddenly I knew. I had all those things. But I'd been rejecting them. The last piece of bark, the last bit of me, to let go of—was the old me." Her head dropped to the table and she sobbed.

Mr. Farley, at her side, reached over and touched her. All the teachers had glistening eyes.

Carol began to speak again. "When I let go of that last bit of bark, I felt free. I felt forgiving. I felt good. I felt God had forgiven me, was making me free of all resentments, envies, even hates. I knew at last, I had received God's grace. Thank you for loving me this year. I'm going home next weekend."

Now she smiled, a radiant smile, full of love, of Christian understanding. If a halo had appeared over her, none of us would have been the least bit surprised.

Dear Lord,

We all know at times we are hurt. We know we often hurt others, however unintentionally.

Teach us Thy Divine love.

When we are selfish,
teach us generosity.

When we have false pride
teach us humility.

As we let go of the lesser
teach us the greater.

We give thanks for
Your constant guidance. Amen.

33—What Shall We Do
With Mr. Pierson?*

Colossians 2:2: *"That their hearts might be comforted, being knit together in love, and unto all riches of the full assurance of understanding, to the acknowledgement of the mystery of God, and the Father, and of Christ."*
I Timothy 6:2: *"And they that have believing masters, let them not despise them, because they are brethren; but rather do them service, because they are faithful and beloved, partakers of the benefit. These things teach and exhort."*
Revelation 7:15: *"Therefore are they before the throne of God, and serve him day and night in his temple: and he that sitteth on the throne shall dwell among them."*

Teachers and parents at the Christian day school always addressed the caretaker respectfully as "Mr. Pierson." But the children, from kindergarten to sixth grade, affectionately called him "Doc." No one could remember how the habit began.

But lately and more frequently, Miss Banks of first grade was asking, "Whatever shall we do with Mr. Pierson?"

Mr. Pierson lived alone in a converted garage at the back of his widowed daughter's home. "I like a place of my own," he explained. He had been hired as full-time caretaker for the

* From *Home Life*, October 1967. Copyright © 1967, The Sunday School Board of the Southern Baptist Convention. All rights reserved. Used by permission.

church and school, and for years, until his arthritis had crippled him so that he needed a cane, he had faithfully performed his duties of mowing lawns, repairing dripping water fountains and trimming his prized geraniums surrounding the buildings.

But the church and school boards had regretfully found it necessary to hire a younger man to operate the power mower and do the janitorial work, permitting Mr. Pierson to work part-time. That way, his dignity would be preserved, and he could earn the tuition for Wanda, his eleven-year-old granddaughter.

Mornings, when the teachers arrived, they knew that Mr. Pierson had already turned on the furnaces or air conditioning as the season demanded. Miss Banks always greeted him politely. "Good morning, Mr. Pierson. How is your arthritis today?" But the children, arriving by bus and car, rushed to him. "Hey, Doc, did ya see the moon eclipse last night on TV?"

Doc Pierson's blue eyes, deep-set in his crunched-in face, lighted. "I sure did, my boy. And say, men, it's a safe guess some of you'll live on that old lady one day!"

Little Dave's ordinarily dull face crinkled into a look of surprise. "Me, Doc?"

Doc's heavy hand rested on the child's head. "Sure thing. A man can do anything he sets his mind to."

A child with a skinned elbow or bumped head ran to Doc for first-aid treatment rather than to his teacher. And if Doc saw a child moping about the playground, he'd say, "Hey, Dickie-boy, your spring's unwound. Come here and let me wind you up."

Mr. Pierson's presence on the playground drove Miss Banks to distraction. Her carefully organized play periods collapsed into chaos as the children mobbed him.

"Doc," third grade Jerry would ask, "What kind of leaf did you say this is?" And he would hold out a geranium leaf.

Doc would take the leaf in his stubby fingers, study its top side, turn it over, then examine the back with a magnifying glass he could always find in his blue shirt pocket. "Hm— m—m, now let me see," he said as though in deep thought. "I'd declare it's a peltate kind. See, it's round and the margins undulate. Most likely, it's geranium."

He put his nose to the leaf and sniffed. "That's right. Now if you look close, then touch it easy like, you'll see veins God put there to feed it. Like the veins he put in every inch of your body. Now, somebody get me an oleander leaf. . . ."

While he waited, Doc would explain about food and water coursing through the veins of leaves and how this geranium leaf would die before its time because it had been taken from the main plant.

Debra rushed up with the requested leaf. Doc fingered it, held it up for his enchanted audience to see. "Now, this here's what we call a lanceolate leaf belonging to the elliptic class. Them's big words for you mites, but it's kinda nice to know 'em. This leaf shows you how God made us all different, yet we eat and drink pretty much alike. Understand?"

Miss Banks, standing on the outer rim of the group, whispered to Mrs. Verder of third. "We try to teach them to say 'them,' not 'em,' and 'nice' not 'kinda nice.' And did you hear him yesterday when they asked him to fix the tether ball? 'I can't now. I ain't et yet,' he said. I know he's good to the children, and he's a good man, but he un-does so much we try to teach them!" She stopped short, overcome with guilt feelings.

Mrs. Verder alternately nodded and shook her head. "He certainly has a way with children."

One rainy day the children arrived at the first grade room at the sound of the bell announcing the end of recess. Their hands were muddy, their clothing water-soaked.

In dismay, Miss Banks asked, "What have you children been doing?"

"We were diggin' for a lizard!" the children yelled in unison. "That Jones kid in fifth pulled off its tail and we wanted to catch it so Doc could fix it. But Doc said the lizard will grow back its tail so it can sit up again!"

"Go wash your hands and scrape the mud off your clothes," commanded Miss Banks in confusion and frustration.

At day's end, she watched Mr. Pierson and Wanda, now in sixth, as they started homeward, hand in hand. The children, waving from bus windows, called, "Bye, Doc. See ya tomorrow!"

The school year ended and with it came graduation night.

The twenty sparkling sixth graders, now leaving the school, were seated in the front rows of the chapel pews. White dresses, fresh curls, white shirts, black ties, and assorted squirmings, gave the assembled parents and teachers mixed emotions of pride and sadness.

Mr. James, principal, congratulated the graduates and reminded them of their Christian education and ideals. The pastor presented them with especially made diplomas.

The ceremonies were about to end, when Mr. Pierson rose from his seat in the back row. "Pastor, if I could, I'd like to say a word."

He mounted the three steps to the podium with difficulty. He waited to catch his breath.

He then spoke in a soft serious tone. "You children in sixth grade, I've watched you grow from kindergarten. We've had a lot of fun. There's just a word I'd like to say to you as a friend. We won't be seeing much of each other from now on.

"But this is what I want to say, and it's something I tell myself every day, especially when the going gets rough. You climb the mountain of your Christian life. There's rocks, there's slick places. You stumble and fall flat on your face.

"What d'ya do? Why, you just get going and pick yourself up. You go on, your eyes on that mountaintop where you know your Lord waits for you. You come to a flat spot and you set yourself down and take a breath, and maybe crawl under a sheltering rock.

"You think maybe, 'This is good enough for me,' but as you set there, something picks at your mind. That's the Lord still calling, reminding you He gave His all for you. Well, now, are you going to do less for Him? So, boys and girls, you get up, dust off your pants and go on. That's the Christian life. That's all I've got to say, except good-bye and the Lord bless and keep you."

Doc Pierson rubbed one hand across his face, and began his slow unsteady descent. But then something happened. Sixth grade rose as though an unseen force propelled each child. They surrounded Doc.

"Good-bye, Doc," they said. "We'll sure miss you. You taught us and helped us a lot. We'll always come back and see you. And if you ever need anything, holler!"

Not even Miss Banks winced at the children saying "holler."

She knew, as did everyone there, the answer to "What shall we do with Mr. Pierson?" He belonged with the school. He was a fine teacher. And Miss Banks silently prayed for strength and wisdom to make herself into the kind of teacher Doc Pierson was.

Dear Lord,

Give us open minds, minds ready to receive and welcome any new lights as it is Your will to reveal to us.

Let us not be bound by custom and habit so that we limit our grasp of opportunities before us.

Give us courage to change our minds and attitudes as lessons are given to us. Help us to be tolerant of the thoughts and deeds of others, and welcome light coming from them. They are Your messengers. We thank You for all Your rich blessings. Amen.

34—The Teacher's Final Report Card

Psalm 25:9: *"The meek will he guide in judgment: and the meek will he teach his way."*
Psalm 25:12: *"What man is he that feareth the Lord? him shall he teach in the way that he shall choose."*
I Corinthians 2:13: *"Which things also we speak, not in the words which man's wisdom teacheth, but which the Holy Ghost teacheth; comparing spiritual things with spiritual."*

I stood in the deserted room. I had given out final report cards to my third graders. The children were gone, and the silence in the room seemed an accusation. Have you been a Christian teacher as well as a teacher this year? How do you rate yourself—A, B, C, D? I felt I must now grade myself.

My mind raced back to September, the beginning of the school year, and the hope I had then for the children in my charge. The children's minds were then filled with memories of summer play. But they had to be brought down to the practicalities of learning. There were sums and takeaways, words to learn to spell along with old-fashioned reading and writing, and all smoothed over with neatness and devotion. I worked to inspire rather than to drive the children to learn.

Nevertheless, I found drawings of stickmen and fantastic dogs scrawled on sheets hidden under books. At times I had failed to maintain interest.

The third graders did go along with reading and writing. But all the while they had big dreams of the young minds.

"I'm going to fly to Mars . . . I'm going to be a teacher like you."

I tried to encourage them with, "Good. That means now is the time to study and learn so you will be ready."

I watched friendships form, then fall apart. I mediated, using Christian ethics to try to put the pieces back together. "Say, 'Bless you,' and you won't be angry with the other person. Did Jesus hit back when people struck him?" Sometimes I failed, sometimes success smiled on us.

There were anxious parents to reassure when they asked, "Why isn't Kim reading better?" "Shouldn't Debra have homework every night?"

"Kim is reading better. But he began school behind the others. Give him time to catch up." "Debra has homework when it is necessary. Let's not overload her now after her illness. We don't want to discourage her."

There were questing minds. "Where is God? How old is He? Where did I come from? Did He write the Bible for us?"

I prayed, "Father, make me wise."

Other times I gave admonitions. "Love your neighbor."

"Who is my neighbor?"

"Your neighbor is the person sitting behind you, in front of you, or beside you." Had I scored there?

"How can I love Jim? He bugs me." That was Joe.

Jim grinned. We knew Joe is a chronic tormenter and Jim had learned to cope with him.

There were quarrels on the playground. I said gently (even while wishing to shake the culprit), "Be kind. Say you are sorry."

"But he hit me first. My dad says to hit back."

Did I dare contradict a parent? I compromised, using Bible lessons. "Did you ever hear of Jesus hitting back?"

There could be no answer to that except no. Again the Christian way was the answer.

Not all was conflict. There was laughter on the playground, and swings flying high. There were slides worn shiny by the seats of thinning jeans. Also there were skinned knees and head bumps, and blood from sensitive noses. Yells: "I'm dying!" I gave assurance, applied band aids and cold compresses.

Christmastime came. There were angels with crooked

halos and dust-bordered sheet robes. There were tears because there could be only one Joseph, one Mary.

Came New Year and resolutions. "What are resolutions?" they asked. I searched my teacher's mind. I prayed, "Help me to make my reply meaningful." The very act of prayer guided me. "I will do better this year. I will help others. I will be kinder to people. Those are resolutions."

"Do you make resolutions, Teacher?"

"Of course."

"What are yours?"

The probing was painful. "To be a better teacher. To be a better Christian."

"But you are—the best."

A halo seemed to settle on my head, but only momentarily. Suddenly bored looks were coming at me. "How long till lunchtime?"

Then came time for achievement tests. The children were tense, wanting to score high. I became tense, too. I wanted so much for them. So that there might be extra to spill over on me? That I might be rated an excellent teacher?

Now the year was over. The last child, clutching books, report card and sweater left over from wintry days, had raced through the door. The buses had rolled away. Even they made tired noises, I mused.

The year had gone out my door too. My students had taken it with them, and all that I had tried to give them.

My favorite poet, Robert Browning said, "What I aspired to be and was not, comforts me." There is much more to teaching than mere teaching. It is being a person who feels and who puts oneself in another person's shoes. There is the recognition of human want and need. The real teacher tries to supply all. She often fails to come up to her expectations of herself more often than not. Yet, she cannot have failed completely, not if she has worked through Christian faith and God's guidance.

I found I could not grade myself. I could only pray alone in an empty room.

Dear Lord,

May the teacher who faces them in the new September

coming up, carry on.

May she feed the seeds I have planted. Replant the barren places I have left.

And, dear Lord, may I then fulfill, with Your constant help, the desires of my own heart in that September, with a new third grade.

May I be the teacher I aspire to be. Amen.